Manderley Prep

A BFF NOVEL

Manderley Prep

CAROL CULVER

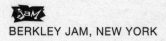

BERKLEY JAM, NEW YORK

THE BERKLEY PUBLISHING GROUP
Published by the Penguin Group
Penguin Group (USA) Inc.
375 Hudson Street, New York, New York 10014, USA
Penguin Group (Canada), 90 Eglinton Avenue East, Suite 700, Toronto, Ontario M4P 2Y3, Canada
(a division of Pearson Penguin Canada Inc.)
Penguin Books Ltd., 80 Strand, London WC2R 0RL, England
Penguin Group Ireland, 25 St. Stephen's Green, Dublin 2, Ireland (a division of Penguin Books Ltd.)
Penguin Group (Australia), 250 Camberwell Road, Camberwell, Victoria 3124, Australia
(a division of Pearson Australia Group Pty. Ltd.)
Penguin Books India Pvt. Ltd., 11 Community Centre, Panchsheel Park, New Delhi—110 017, India
Penguin Group (NZ), 67 Apollo Drive, Rosedale, North Shore 0632, New Zealand
(a division of Pearson New Zealand Ltd.)
Penguin Books (South Africa) (Pty.) Ltd., 24 Sturdee Avenue, Rosebank, Johannesburg 2196,
South Africa

Penguin Books Ltd., Registered Offices: 80 Strand, London WC2R 0RL, England

This book is an original publication of The Berkley Publishing Group.

FIRST EDITION: December 2007

Library of Congress Cataloging-in-Publication Data

Culver, Carol, 1936–
    Manderley Prep : a BFF novel / Carol Culver.—1st ed.
      p. cm.
    Summary: Cindy Ellis lives with her wealthy stepmother, who forces her to work for minimum
wage at her upscale spa, and her two stepsisters who either ignore her or mercilessly taunt her, but
when Cindy gets a scholarship to attend Manderley Prep and she meets the great-looking Italian
exchange student, it looks like her life might start to improve.
    ISBN 978-0-425-21747-4
    [1. Stepfamilies—Fiction. 2. Preparatory schools—Fiction. 3. High schools—Fiction.
4. Schools—Fiction. 5. Self-confidence—Fiction.] I. Title.
    PZ7.C906Man 2007

[Fic]—dc22
                                        2007031788

PRINTED IN THE UNITED STATES OF AMERICA

10 9 8 7 6 5 4 3 2 1

one

I have never let my schooling interfere with my education.

—Mark Twain

Last night Cindy dreamed she went to Manderley again. In the morning her stepsisters yelled, "Wake up, Orphan Girl," and she knew this time it was no dream. Starting today she was a junior at Manderley Prep, the most exclusive, expensive high school in the Bay Area, maybe in the whole state of California. No longer would she go to Castle High with its crowded pre-fab classrooms, its tired, overworked teachers and tuned-out, stoned students. As a poor scholarship girl, she might not fit in with the rich kids at Manderley, but she'd never really fit in anywhere anyway. So what?

Since she'd overslept, Cindy had no time to apply concealer

1

to her face or grab an energy bar. Not that she had zits; it was the freckles she wanted to hide. And there was no way she could have gotten anything into her stomach before ten A.M. without gagging. But still. She threw on a pair of secondhand jeans she'd found at the Goodwill store and a T-shirt with a faded Dutch Goose logo, and grabbed her backpack and her clarinet. Brie and Lauren were already out of the house and impatiently honking the horn of their Jeep Cherokee.

"Next time you're late, we're not waiting for you. You can take the bus," Brie said.

"Sorry," Cindy muttered. They'd love an excuse to ditch her in the morning, but their mother, Irina, made them give her a ride to school and to her job at Irina's day spa after school.

"Well, look at her," Lauren said to Brie as Cindy dragged her clarinet case with her into the backseat. "If it isn't Benny fucking Goodman."

Cindy almost dropped her backpack in surprise. Not because her sister had used the f word, but because she'd even heard of the world's greatest clarinet player.

"Who is he, anyway? I saw his name on your old sweat-shirt. Some rock star?" Lauren jabbed Brie in the arm and laughed hysterically. Then her laughter died. "Hey, isn't that my shirt?"

"You threw it away," Cindy said. But Lauren didn't hear her. Not with the music blasting from their new sound system. A few minutes later Lauren turned her head to look at Cindy again. Her perfectly straightened blond hair brushed against her spray-on-tanned cheekbone.

"Just do me a favor and don't tell anyone at school you're related to us, which you're really not."

"Don't worry," Cindy said. They thought she'd claim to be any part of the family her father had married into? As if.

Maybe Cindy would live to regret the day she'd filled out those scholarship forms. Now she'd be at the same school where her mean, self-centered sisters were seniors, members of the popular clique and cheerleaders. And they thought she'd claim to be related to those bitchy girls? Not in this lifetime.

"You're not going to like it there," Lauren said, as if she'd read Cindy's mind. "Everyone's rich and snobby. If you don't wear the right clothes or drive the right car, you're nobody. Of course in your case you've always been nobody, so maybe you won't notice."

Cindy fastened her seat belt and pressed her spine into the corner of the backseat where she was wedged between a stack of tank top and miniskirt cheerleader uniforms and blue and gold pom-poms. She felt the chill from their cold warnings right through her T-shirt.

"Even Brie and I had a little trouble fitting in at first," Lauren continued.

"Then why . . ."

"Why do we go there?" Lauren lit a cigarette and blew a stream of smoke into the backseat. At least they weren't smoking pot today and filling the car with that sweet, sickly smell of weed that would cling to Cindy's clothes. They bragged to Cindy that the latest shipment they'd gotten from south of the border was the best they'd ever had. She'd seen them hide their stash under the seat cushions of the jeep in snack-sized Baggies Irina bought in bulk at Costco.

Lauren answered her own question. "I'll tell you why. It's the cool school, that's why."

Lauren must not have noticed the way Cindy's lip curled down at the corner, not that she noticed anything about Cindy except when she was wearing her hand-me-downs, because she went on and on about Manderley.

"And the football team is number one in the private school league," Brie added.

Cindy knew her sisters thought their chants and stunts, during which they took every opportunity to shake their booty at halftime, played a huge part in the football team's ranking. They made no secret of the fact that they spent time on the sidelines lusting over the jocks in their tight Lycra pants. After the games they did more than just lust, unless they were only bragging.

"And they're teaching Chinese this year," Lauren said. "Because of the new headmaster. He thinks the Chinese are taking over the world. We either nuke 'em or we learn their language."

Cindy's mouth fell open. "So you're taking Chinese?"

Lauren rolled her eyes at Cindy's obvious cluelessness. "No, dumb-ass. Don't you know Chinese is the hardest language to learn? Why would I do that and lower my GPA? I'm trying to explain to you why Manderley is such a cool school. Are you listening?"

How could she not be listening? She was a captive audience, stuck in the backseat surrounded by secondhand smoke.

"Of course it's a cool campus too."

Cindy couldn't disagree with Lauren on that. At the center of the grounds was the old mansion once owned by Gertrude Manderley, early California feminist and poet. Surrounded by green lawns, playing fields, old gnarled trees and new buildings all named after some rich alum, like the George C. Effington Family Auditorium. At orientation she'd noticed every corner, every brick and every stone had a name attached to it, like the Mayard Phillips III Drinking Fountain. It had to be really old because these days who needed to drink water from a fountain when everyone carried their own personal bottle of spring water.

"But mostly it's about meeting the right people."

Cindy knew where Lauren got that idea. That was Irina's theme song. It was why she'd sunk so much money into her string of upscale day spas so she herself could buy her way into Silicon Valley society and meet the right people. Specifically Husband Number Three.

Brie chimed in. "And getting into the right college. Which

will be no problem if our cheerleading squad makes it to the finals this year and we get noticed by certain recruiters. We'll have our pick of all the top schools."

Cindy bit her tongue. She'd seen her sisters' SAT scores, and cheerleading stars or not, they'd be lucky to get into Chico State, the infamous party school. If things went as she planned, she'd show them who got into the "right" college.

Her goal was to go as far away as possible, preferably somewhere on the East Coast, and never come back. She knew the drill now. Knew how to fill out the application forms herself, forge the required signatures and write the kind of essay it took to get financial aid. How many clarinet playing, penniless orphans could there be applying to Harvard, Yale and Princeton?

She wasn't at all afraid to play the orphan card to get what she wanted. Ever since her father died, she'd felt like she was completely on her own. Legally she had a guardian—Irina—who provided a roof over her head and three meals a day and who gave her a job at her spa so she could earn spending money.

But emotionally she had no support from her stepmother or her stepsisters. They wouldn't miss her when she was eighteen and gone off on her own, and God knew she wouldn't miss them. In the meantime she was making plans for her future, which began today with a prep school education as a stepping stone to success.

Lauren turned around to sing along to the radio. Cindy

stared at the back of her head and wondered for the thousandth time how her quirky, low-key father had ever ended up
with their high-maintenance mother.

Twenty minutes later Brie jerked the jeep to a halt in front
of the white stone mansion Gertrude Manderley's patron had
built for her a century ago.

"Get out here," Brie said. "Before we park. And remember,
you don't know us and we don't know you."

Cindy slid across the seat and was lifting her clarinet out of
the car when Brie started pulling away. She caught her instrument before the battered case bounced on the pavement. One
minute sooner and it would have been her butt bouncing on
the pavement.

Lauren stuck her head out of the window. "Be out here in
front of the quad at four-thirty," she called before they drove
to the parking lot. "Something comes up, we'll call you. Got
your phone?"

Cindy nodded and slung her backpack over her shoulder.
Other kids were getting out of their sixteenth-birthday-present
Beemers or H2 Hummers. She shivered in the cool morning
air. She wasn't at Castle anymore, with her Best Friends Forever, though she still wore the gold necklace with the dangling
letter F. Lizzie wore the B and Georgie wore the other F. If she
were at Castle she'd know where to eat lunch, who to eat with
and who to avoid.

She took a deep breath and inhaled the scent of new grass

and old money. Yes, this was a different world from her old school, where the smell of exhaust fumes from the nearby freeway blended with the aroma of tacos from the lunch wagon parked in front of the school.

Instead of boys dressed like surfer dudes (though few of them ever went to Santa Cruz to ride the waves), here the guys were totally outfitted in Abercrombie from top to toe. Girls at Castle were still into the bare midriff with the pierced navel. At Manderley a quick glance told her the girls wore layered tank tops, short skirts and flip-flops or even a sundress.

She'd never fit in. Never fit into size two designer jeans even if she could afford them. Never. What had she done? No matter how challenging the classes, how inspiring the teachers, she wasn't prepared for the shaft of loneliness that struck her as friends greeted friends with shrieks and hugs after a long summer break. Oh, she might put on a brave face in front of her stepsisters, but at heart she was not a loner like her father. She needed friends. She missed her friends. Especially Lizzie.

Unable to quell the hollow sinking feeling in the pit of her stomach, Cindy scanned the crowd, trying to pretend she was waiting for someone. Anyone.

Just when she thought she couldn't fake it another minute, a black vintage Alfa Romeo convertible slowly cruised by. At the wheel was a bronze god. That was the only way to describe him.

"Who . . . is . . . that?" a girl on the sidewalk asked breathlessly.

"Some movie star?"

"You got the star part right. He's the Italian prince the soccer coach recruited."

"A prince came to play soccer for Manderley?"

Cindy strained to hear the answer but other louder voices drowned her out.

The prince wore dark sunglasses. His skin was the color of warm copper. His hair was as black as obsidian. Cindy stood rooted in place, staring as he drove past. If the first bell had rung she wouldn't have heard it. If the earth shook she wouldn't have felt it.

What she did feel was waves of heat rising from the sidewalk, traveling through her body until she was hot all over, making her face flame and her heart pound. Her sisters, who talked nonstop about the guys they'd slept with or given blow jobs to, or wished they'd slept with or wished they hadn't given blow jobs to, had never mentioned a soccer star. They'd never mentioned a Greek god in a sports car. And they would have if they'd seen him first. But they hadn't. She had.

A hush fell over the crowd of students as the Alfa turned, and just before it did, the guy turned his head, raised one hand in a half salute, half wave. Cindy couldn't help it. Her arm lifted all by itself and she waved back.

Why? He wasn't waving at her. How could he be? She didn't know him and he didn't know her. From somewhere behind her she heard the unmistakable sound of girls snickering.

Had someone seen her making a fool of herself? On her first day? Oh, please no.

She dropped her arm like it was made of lead and stuffed her hand into her pocket. The Alfa continued on the circular drive on out toward the parking lot. No more snickers. Just silence. It was as if the whole school was holding its collective breath until he disappeared into the mass of expensive parked cars.

He was gone and life went back to normal. For everyone but her. Shouts, cries and laughter filled the air. She must have been the only one who'd waved at him like he was her friend or something. Now she felt like some kind of clueless dimwit.

Cindy didn't dare look around to see if anyone was staring at her. She swallowed hard and glanced at her watch like being on time for class was her biggest concern. It was eight-thirty, but no bell rang. Did they really expect students to get to class on time if they didn't ring a bell?

Was personal responsibility the real difference between Castle and Manderley? Cindy pulled her schedule out of her backpack, turned and went to look for her locker. All by herself.

two

School's a weird thing, I'm not sure it works.

—Johnny Depp

Toby Hatcher (no relation to Teri) slipped into a seat in the back of the U.S. history class about a half hour late just as Mr. Schaffer started listing the groups he had chosen for the semester projects. Each group got a period of the twentieth century to research. Brian Foster, who'd been on Prozac since freshman year, and a geek named Todd got the Depression. How perfect was that? A girl he knew from Frisbee on the green and Joe Diamond got the sixties, and after everyone in class had been named, Schaffer stopped and scanned the room until his gaze came to rest on Toby.

"Mr. Hatcher, how nice of you to make it today," Schaffer

said, his voice dripping with sarcasm. "You will be doing your report on World War Two, if that meets with your approval, with . . ." He looked down at his sheet. "Cindy Ellis."

Cindy Ellis? Who the hell was that? Where was his friend Rich? He was supposed to team up with Rich. Rich would be the ideal partner because he'd do all the work. Toby glanced around the room. No Richard, but he did see a girl in the front row he'd never seen before turn and give him a funny look. Who would sit in the front row if they weren't some dorky loser? Just as well. He didn't need any more girl hassles. Not after what he'd been through.

"Just as important as the twenty-page paper you'll be writing is the oral presentation. Of course, PowerPoint is acceptable."

After class Cindy caught up with him at the door.

"Are you Toby?"

"Uh . . . yeah."

"So we're going to be working together, I guess."

"Yeah, I guess I should give you my number. So, uh, we can call each other, in case . . ." In case what? Maybe he could drop the class or at least change the topic to something more current than World War II, like the rap music of today. But how would he get out of working with this girl when Rich showed up?

He looked over her shoulder, hoping to find his friend and switch partners, but she was looking at him with intense bright blue eyes as if he was some kind of idiot. He did feel like he was brain-dead and maybe it showed. After an awkward silence she spoke.

"I'll give you mine."

They wrote down numbers, stood for a second, then bumped into each other while walking out the door. He stood back and said, "Sorry."

He *was* sorry. Sorry he'd come to school at all the first day. Sorry he'd gotten paired with a strange, tall, redheaded girl; sorry his head felt like it was somewhere else; sorry that he had to write a boring paper on a boring war no one even remembered.

three

Piu che le parole persuadano gli esempi. *Actions speak louder than words.*

—Italian proverb

Cindy was angrily stuffing her history books back into her locker, wondering what else could go wrong on the first day of the rest of her life, when her clarinet popped out of her arm onto the ground.

"I believe you have dropped your clarinetto," he said in a deep, dark, heavily accented voice.

She whirled around.

No dark glasses. Nothing to cover those sexy, heavy-lidded eyes this time. But she would have known him anywhere. He was the prince and he was standing there holding her clarinet.

"Oh . . . thank you. Yes, that's mine." Nothing like stating the obvious. Of course it was hers. He knew it. She knew it. She grabbed it out of his hand and shoved the worn leather case back into her locker.

"Perhaps you can tell me where is the music room then."

Her mind raced. She'd seen the band room but she couldn't remember. She was so rattled she couldn't remember her own name. But he hadn't asked her name, so it didn't really matter. "I . . . uh . . . I don't know." Her voice trembled. "I'm new here myself."

"Like me." He gave her a slow conspiratorial smile.

Like him? There was nobody like him.

"I'm coming from Italy just for a few days and I'm always lost." She didn't know a macho guy could shrug like that or admit he was lost, but he did. "Then I see you and I notice you are bringing your . . . how do you say, clarinetto to school, and this means they may have the jazz music here at school."

"Yes." Cindy's hands were shaking so much she dropped the math textbook she was holding. "They do. But I'm not actually in the band. Not yet. There may be tryouts for it, I don't know."

He picked her book up and handed it to her. His knuckles brushed her palm. His face was so close she could see flecks of green in his dark eyes. She tried to say thank you, but it came out like a wheeze.

He leaned against her locker. "I don't know too. But I know I love the American jazz. But you think I must do these tryouts?"

"Maybe. What do you play?"

"Piano. I would like to play like your Teddy Wilson and Oscar Peterson."

Piano. A soccer-playing jazz pianist who looked like he stepped out of one of those European fashion magazines at her stepmother's spa, *and* who knew who the great piano players were? Was she still dreaming? If she'd had a free hand, she would have pinched herself.

"But I have not had the lessons, you know. Maybe I'm not good enough for the band."

Make that a *modest*, soccer-playing jazz pianist. Now she knew she was dreaming.

"Oh, I'm sure you must be, I mean if you . . . if you're . . ." What was wrong with her? English was her native language and yet she couldn't seem to spit out an entire sentence. She glanced at her watch.

"I am keeping you from your class. *Addio*, then," he said and with a wave he was gone.

Somehow Cindy managed to gather the right books, close and lock her locker, only to start walking to her English class in the totally wrong direction.

four

After she turned around, Cindy checked her schedule and realized she had a free period before English. She walked out onto the quiet leafy campus and sat down on the Joyce and Eric Barber Stone Bench. When she flipped open her cell phone she saw a text message from Lizzie filled with the usual first-day angst.

Cindy punched in Lizzie's cell number. Now was not the time for text messaging. She needed to talk to her friend and give her the usual first-day-back-at-school pep talk.

"Where are you?" Cindy asked.

"In my car. I've had it. I can't take it anymore. I'm outta here."

"Already? Come on, Liz, you can do it. Go back inside and go to class. You'll get used to it. You always do."

"I always had you around before," Lizzie said. "Tell me about Manderley. What have they got, valet parking, complimentary hot breakfast, and free massages? They should for what they're charging. Some people have all the luck."

"Luck? You call this luck? At Castle I never got assigned a history partner who thinks I'm a dork and that I'll do all the work on the project for him. At Castle I never had to spend all day at school with my snotty stepsisters only to see them at home after school. And I never noticed that everyone in the whole school was richer than God, because even if they were they wouldn't throw it in my face. And nobody ever laughed at me for waving to someone I don't know."

"Well if you put it that way . . ."

"There's no other way to put it."

"Then you're coming back?"

"I can't. I'm stuck."

"Met any guys yet?" Lizzie asked hopefully.

"A guy named Toby." No way was she going to mention the Italian. She didn't even know his name. And she might never see him again.

"What does he look like?"

"Who?"

"Toby!"

"He looks like he just got out of bed. He's got this vacant

look in his eyes that tells me he's spaced out and high on something. I know the type. If I don't do all the work on the project, he'll drag my grade down. Oh, yeah, I met a guy. But I wish I hadn't."

"Come on, what does he really look like?"

"Remember how Jake Gyllenhaal looked in *The Good Girl*? Well, that's what this Toby looks like."

"He looks like Jake Gyllenhaal? Ohmygod, that is so cool. Wait till I tell Georgie and everyone."

Cindy shook her head. She should never have mentioned Toby or Jake Gyllenhaal. Now Lizzie still envied her even after what she'd said. Lizzie had begged her parents to send her to Manderley but they couldn't afford the $28,000 a year. Not if they wanted to eat on a regular basis.

"Don't tell anyone but Georgie. This is between the BFF. You wouldn't like it here, Liz. You know my sisters? Imagine a whole school full of them and you'll get the idea."

"I thought it would be better, you know."

"It's not better," Cindy assured her. "It's just . . . different."

She wished her friend could spend a day there. She'd go running happily back to Castle. Because Manderley was just another school—a little cleaner, a little smaller, a lot richer, but filled with kids who were also stumbling through the halls on their way to class the way they'd soon be stumbling through life. And one Italian, who even though he claimed he might be lost, probably knew his way around the world just fine.

"Then I feel sorry for you," Lizzie said.

"Don't!" Cindy said. If there was anything she hated, it was pity. She'd do anything to avoid it, even lying.

"But I do. Because even though you've got a Jake Gyllenhaal look-alike, you haven't got your best friends."

"That's right," Cindy conceded. "But I'm okay. Really. I'll be fine." Liz was right. She had no best friends at school and no real family at home. No longer was her father tinkering in the garage, hoping to invent something to make them rich. That dream finally came true. At least it made Irina rich when he died and she inherited all his money. The dream that didn't come true was thinking Irina would blend their families into one big happy whole.

"I've gotta go now," Cindy said soberly. "Talk to you later."

A few minutes later she was walking behind two senior girls who were friends of Brie and Lauren. They didn't notice her. No one did. With her red hair and her nearly six feet of height, you'd think she'd be hard to miss. Not at Manderley. Here she was invisible.

"How was your summer?" one asked the other.

"Borrring."

"I saw you with Parker at the Bridge concert."

"I *so* did not want to be there. She's such a geek. But her father got us tickets. What could I say?"

"No?"

"No! Besides, Trevor went on this stupid five-hundred-mile charity ride with Lance Armstrong. His butt still hurts. He thinks he might be impotent. I said he shouldn't worry, that way he won't have to wear condoms anymore."

"Do you care?"

The girl shrugged. "Why should I?"

Cindy hurried past them, but she couldn't move far enough from the inane conversation going on there and everywhere else on this campus today. She felt a rush of blood to the head, and swear to God, she was that close to running out the front door of the school and down the street to the Starbucks for a double decaf latte and then taking her clarinet and hopping on a bus to go back to Castle where her friends were. Where they'd welcome her with open arms. NOT. She could not throw away everything because of a few shallow girls. Even a whole school full of shallow girls.

Of course she didn't leave. The shaking hands, the knocking knees and the inability to speak clearly were just minor symptoms she would get over. She knew what was wrong with her. It was Culture Shock. She was a stranger in a strange land.

She'd wanted to go there. She would give it a chance. Never mind the classes were so far just so-so and the kids were obnoxious. She'd gotten her wish. She never looked back. She never cut class. She never quit anything. She wasn't that kind of girl.

five

A free lunch is found only in mousetraps.

—John Capozzi

At noon in the cafeteria the sight of the salad bar, sushi bar and steam trays filled with teen favorites like mac and cheese made Cindy feel nauseous. It wasn't the food—it was the fear of eating alone. There was no complimentary hot breakfast, but the lunch was included in the tuition. She couldn't get sick today. She'd have no way to get home. Irina was at work and if she came to get Cindy, she'd take her to work and make her help out at the spa as she'd done all summer.

She supposed there must be a school nurse at Manderley. If someone got sick there, they'd have their housekeeper come and get them. Their mother would be busy playing tennis and their father was probably power-lunching at one of the gourmet Google cafeterias.

The rich cheesy smell of the macaroni and cheese reminded her of her father. He used to make it for her when her mother was sick. He'd come in from the garage, cook something for them and go back to work for hours, driven by the will to succeed. A will that Cindy hoped she'd inherited.

She was proud of him for sticking to it later when her stepmother told him to get a "real" job. Now all she had left of him were the memories, the precious clarinet he'd left her and his love of swing music.

Cindy piled some lettuce on her plate and ladled on some fat-free dressing. Amazing what you could get for $28,000 a year. Back at Castle there'd be dried-up chicken tenders oozing trans fats and calories, and they'd cost five dollars.

Now came the moment she'd been dreading all summer: looking pathetic by eating lunch by herself. She headed for a table in the corner and as soon as she sat down, an exotic looking girl with straight shiny black hair cut in layers and with stylish glasses framing her almond-shaped eyes put her tray on the table and quietly slid into the seat across from her.

"Is this seat taken?" she asked.

"Now it is," Cindy said with a smile. Usually when a person was that beautiful she never had to ask permission to sit down. Maybe the girl didn't know what she looked like. Cindy couldn't believe she didn't have any friends to sit with.

Thank God she didn't. On Cindy's first day she wasn't eating alone after all. It didn't matter that she'd never seen this girl before and might never see her again. Life suddenly looked a lot brighter.

"Can I ask you a question?" the girl asked in a slight accent, part British, part Chinese, part East-Coast American. Where was she from, anyway?

Cindy nodded. *Anything. Just don't get up and move when your friends arrive.*

The girl reached into her Coach bag and pulled out a handful of parking tickets.

Cindy gasped. The name on the tickets was Victoria Lee. "Are you Victoria?"

She nodded. "Almost every day I find one on my car. Why? What did I do wrong?"

"You parked in a no-parking zone." Cindy said. "Maybe just the wrong side of the street."

"I didn't see any sign. And in Hong Kong you can park wherever you find a place."

You're not in Hong Kong anymore, Cindy thought. "You need to pay the fines or you'll be arrested," she told Victoria.

Victoria gasped. "Arrested? Oh, no, can't I just pay someone off? That's what we do at home."

"You could try, but it probably wouldn't work. You'd get arrested for trying to bribe an officer."

"Okay." Victoria slowly put the tickets back in her bag.

24

Cindy wasn't sure the girl understood the gravity of the situation. "You should take care of it today," she said. "Have you been here long?"

"I came this summer."

"You speak English very well."

"Thank you. I should. My father's American and I went to an international school in Hong Kong. I wanted to stay there with my friends, but my parents decided to invest in California property, so they sent me here to live in the house they bought. Then they went back. My mother wants to live close to her family and my father . . ." Victoria bit her lip and looked down at her sandwich. "I've been told by certain people that I have a tendency to overshare with strangers. I hope I haven't bored you with the details of my life."

"No, not at all. I'm new too. You mean you live alone?"

"For now, but my parents are going to hire a housekeeper. Actually I'm getting used to being on my own," she said a little defensively.

"So am I," Cindy murmured. Now who was oversharing with a stranger? Maybe it was because she *was* a complete stranger.

"Where are your parents?" Victoria asked.

"They're dead."

"I'm sorry. Then you know what it's like to live alone."

"No." *Unfortunately.* "I live with my stepmother and step-sisters."

25

"You have sisters? You're lucky. I've always wanted a sister."

"These are *step*sisters. We're not really related at all. What happened was their mother married my father. That's how I got them."

"Oh, I see. How many do you have?"

"Two. Two too many," Cindy added lightly.

Victoria nodded but she looked puzzled. Maybe in Hong Kong people's fathers didn't marry witches with two awful daughters. Or if they did, the father's daughter kept her mouth shut about how she felt about the new additions to the family. Usually Cindy did keep her mouth shut and never complained, but there was something about Victoria that caused her to say what she felt.

A certain awareness showed in the way Victoria looked at Cindy. "There's an old Chinese story my grandmother told me about a girl who lived with her stepmother and stepsisters," she said. "They were very mean to her."

"Really?" Cindy asked faintly. Maybe the Cinderella story was a universal myth. If only it was just a myth. Unfortunately Cindy was forced to live out the reality of the myth every day in every way. She didn't want to act too interested in case Victoria felt compelled to launch into the story, and then Cindy would have to pretend she'd never heard it before and it had no bearing whatsoever on Cindy's life.

On the other hand, since Cindy really shouldn't be talking about her family problems anyway, maybe she should just let her tell it and hope it had the requisite happy ending. "How does it go?"

"A poor girl named Yeh-Shen who lived with her wicked step-mother and her sisters had nothing, no clothes and no friends, until she got a beautiful azure outfit made from magic fish bones."

"Fish bones?" Cindy asked. This was not the same story. Or perhaps there was something lost in translation. "It must have been kind of scratchy," she murmured.

"You're right," Victoria said. "But Yeh-Shen only cared about how she looked, not how she felt. She had to have the beautiful azure clothes as well as golden slippers to wear to the feast where she could choose a husband. But along the way she lost one of her slippers."

"I think I know how this ends," Cindy said just as a group of loud-mouthed girls descended on their table, plunked their trays down and, ignoring Victoria and Cindy, proceeded to trade first-day-back-at-school experiences.

"Have you seen the new headmaster?" one girl asked the others.

"Not yet. All I know is his name is Kavanaugh. My parents said Mr. Gregory got fired for being too easy. We'd better not have a dress code," the girl said, tugging at her bra strap, "or I'm outta here."

"Yeah, where to? Castle?"

The others burst into derisive laughter until the first girl dropped her fork and stared off across the room.

"There he is," she announced, halfway out of her seat.

"Who, the new headmaster?" her friend asked, grabbing her glasses and swiveling around in her chair.

"No, you idiot," the girl hissed. "Stop staring."

Since she wasn't talking to her, Cindy turned around and stared. The room was full of kids. She had no idea who they were talking about.

"Oh my God, he is so hot."

"Who?" another girl asked, getting up from her chair to get a better look.

Her friend yanked her back into her seat.

"The Italian exchange student. The soccer dude. And he's all alone. I could cry."

"What are you doing?"

"I'm waving to him. I can't stand to see someone eat by himself."

Cindy craned her neck and looked around the room. Her eyes widened. Her heart rate jumped. It was him again. This time she had a full frontal view of him from a safe distance. And time to notice he was wearing an unlined jacket, like the kind she'd only seen in fashion magazines, over a sexy black T-shirt, straight-leg jeans and smooth leather shoes probably straight off the Via Veneto. As different from the all-American boys in their flip-flops, baggy shorts and T-shirts as a Ferrari was from a Ford. And this Ferrari was heading straight for their table.

six

Lord, confound this surly sister,
Blight her brow with blotch and blister,
Cramp her larynx, lung and liver,
In her guts a galling give her.

—J. M. Synge

"Hey, is that your little sister?" Bo Bradley cut in the cafeteria line at Manderley and helped himself to a handful of fries from Lauren Vanderhoffer's tray.

"Who?"

"The redhead. Sitting over there in the corner."

"Who cares?"

Bo shrugged. "A friend of mine wants to know."

Lauren looked over his shoulder at Bo's homies, who were sharing a joint on the lawn outside the cafeteria. One thing about Manderley, it was a closed campus, but weed was always available in the parking lot. Good thing, otherwise they'd have to buy it on a street corner on the east side of the freeway and God knows what kind of shit they were selling.

It was probably one of those stoned-out losers who wanted to know about Cindy. But why? No guy had ever shown any interest in her that Lauren knew. And Cindy wasn't interested in guys. All she cared about was . . . well, who knew what she cared about. And who cared, really?

"If your *friend* is referring to Cindy Ellis," Lauren said, her pert chin tilted at a haughty angle, "she isn't my sister except by a freak of circumstances."

"Whaddya mean, she's not your sister?" he asked with his mouth full of potato. "I saw you come to school in the same car. You live in the same house, right?"

Lauren didn't answer. Instead she gave him a karate chop to the wrist when he reached for another fry.

"Yeeow," he said.

"You can tell anyone who asks about Cindy that she's got a social disease and she isn't interested in guys anyway."

His eyes widened. "You mean . . ."

Lauren nodded and headed toward a table where Brie and her boyfriend, Amos, were drinking cans of Red Bull they'd smuggled in inside their backpacks. The school had a "no high-fructose corn syrup" policy, but it was hard to enforce.

Lauren slammed her tray on the table. "I've had it with orphan girl."

Brie looked up. "What did she do now?"

Lauren took a deep breath. "It's nothing she did, it's just the way she is. Since she transferred, everyone knows she's connected to us—how, I don't know. But some teacher asked me about her. And the soccer coach. Now some retard is asking about her. Don't ask me why. Maybe he recognized her from his support group. I'm gonna get a sign that reads, 'Questions about Cindy will be forwarded to an automatic answering machine. I'm not related to her. I haven't seen her and I don't have her number. Give it a rest,' and wear it around my neck. Just because *our* mother happened to marry her father doesn't mean Cindy is *our* sister."

"The same thing happened to me," Brie said. "Here's what I do. I go, 'Thanks for asking. Now go screw yourself and leave me alone.' "

Brie bit into her grilled cheese sandwich and chewed it loudly like she'd gotten hold of one of Cindy's arms.

When her phone rang her new favorite ring tone, Brie glanced at the caller ID and made a face.

"Yeah, what?" she snapped into the phone.

"I need you both to help me after school," her mother said. "I've got a full schedule at the salon today. All the Laguna Vista housewives are into keeping up their summer tans starting today."

"We've got cheerleading practice, and we can't miss that. Good news—we're definitely going to be co-captains this year. I mean, who else but us? It won't be you-know-who, who spent the summer at fat camp because she came home fatter than ever."

"Who's that?"

"Mom, I'm in the cafeteria. I can't mention any names, someone might hear me. Anyway this certain person was already too heavy to jump more than two inches off the ground before she went to that camp. And it can't be a certain person who thinks she's God's gift to Manderley cheerleading now that she's had a nose job. Because guess what? There're more important things than a perfect nose, like maybe being capable of doing a back handspring? Yeah, we'll definitely get it for sure if the team has any sense and Ms. Lard-Ass doesn't screw us over."

"I thought Cammie Bowles was the captain."

"She was until she fell off the pyramid during the final home game last year. What a klutz. Surprised it never happened before. Everyone told her she should be a base. What are we, her personal support staff? They thought she was okay, but it turns out she cracked her neck vertebra. We just heard she'll be watching from the sidelines in a neck brace this year. Bad news for her, good news for us. So we're busy today and every day after school practicing and lining up the other girls to vote for us for co-captains. We should get it. We deserve to get it. We know more routines than anyone especially you-know-who-I-mean who thinks she can get by because she's fucking the football coach."

"What?"

"Don't tell anyone I said that. It may not be true. But it probably is. Since she had her picture in *Cheerleading Today* she's been a total bitch. When we're captains it's a cinch things will be different. We'll call the shots. We'll decide who does what routine and then we get the big scholarship for next year, wherever we want to go—UCLA, USC . . ."

"Really?" Irina said.

"Yes, really. So get Cindy. She doesn't need to join the band or whatever else she thinks she's going to do. Band is for dorks anyway. Yeah, get Cindy."

"I tried calling her but she didn't answer. This is important. I don't want to have to hire someone to help me."

"Try again." Brie craned her neck. Cindy was nowhere to be seen. "She's probably gone to the computer lab to play Nancy Drew games by herself. What a pathetic loser. And now . . ." She heaved a huge heavy sigh. "We gotta see her every day."

seven

Italians were eating with a knife and fork when the French were still eating each other. The Medici family had to bring their Tuscan cooks up there so they could make something edible.

—Mario Batali

Marco Valenti walked through the cafeteria of Manderley Prep holding a tray with a sloppy sandwich and a bowl of so-called minestrone soup. He looked around at the kids in their tattered blue jeans and the plastic shoes they wore, which were hardly shoes at all, and felt a shaft of revulsion hit him like a soccer ball kicked at his gut. It wasn't just the slobs, it was the food they were eating.

He had yet to have a good meal since he'd moved there from Italy to live with his aunt and uncle last month. It wasn't their fault. It was just that he hardly ever saw them. They were busy and so was he. They ate in high-class restaurants; he ate hamburgers at the In-N-Out or whatever he found in their refrigerator. There were no long, lively family dinners with five courses. Apparently no one in America had time for that.

The house his relatives lived in was huge—what did they call them in English? A McMansion? And they didn't even have any servants except for a cleaning service that came once a week. Sure, it was nice, but nothing compared to the ancestral home of the Dukes of Savoy where his family lived in Tuscany.

All that history and all that money. Sometimes Marco felt it weighing him down like a load of Carrera marble. In California he felt free. Free to spend money on anything he wanted, like a new car. Free to fall in love with California and the California girls with their blond hair and their perfect bodies. Good food and people wearing the latest styles could wait.

For one year he'd give up eating cannolis and linguini arrabbiata and drinking limoncello. Instead he'd eat hamburgers and do whatever he wanted without his father looking over his shoulder. If he spent more money than his father gave him, he'd earn his own playing online poker. It was almost too easy. Just last night he'd made fifteen hundred dollars.

He felt a warm sweaty hand clamp down on his shoulder.

"Hi, Coach," he said.

Oh, hell, he'd missed soccer practice this morning. He couldn't get up at seven. Not after staying up half the night playing Texas Hold 'Em. No one in Italy practiced soccer at such an ungodly hour. They couldn't expect him to get out of bed just to run around a field with a bunch of boys who couldn't score a goal if the goalie fell over dead.

"Missed you this morning, Marco."

"Sorry. I had a family, how do you say, urgency? Something about my visa was not regular so I had to take care of. Don't worry, I'll be coming there after school."

The coach slapped him on the back. "Want to talk to you about something else," he said. "Wondered how you felt about coaching the girls soccer team?"

"Girls?" he said. "Girls play soccer here?"

The coach laughed. "I know. I know. We all wish they'd just do the cheerleading thing, if they have to do anything, but it's something about the Manderley woman's endowment and that Title Nine crap."

Marco had no idea what he was talking about. Why did Americans talk so fast?

"Never mind," the coach said. "Just think about it." Then he said something about how they were counting on him to power them into the championships this year.

"The new headmaster is gung ho about sports, which means more money for the team. We've even got a new van to transport the players in comfort. Multiple cup holders, navigation system, MP3 players, video—you name it, we've got it."

Marco nodded and started toward the far corner of the room where some girl was waving to him. He'd never seen her before but what the hell, it was better than eating with a guy named Joe he'd met last week at orientation for new students. He'd made the mistake of asking Joe where the discos were.

"Discos? You mean like clubs? You gotta go to the city to SoMa, but they'll card you."

"What's that?"

"Ask you for ID. Legally you can't drink here until you're twenty-one."

What kind of country was this anyway? Sure, maybe Italians consumed a lot of alcohol, but no one he knew had any problem. In his country kids learned to drink at home. Alcohol abuse wasn't tolerated. Sex was something else he didn't understand about America. Joe and his friends talked nonstop about getting laid. He suspected most of them were virgins from what they said.

"So what do you guys do for fun?" he'd asked just to be polite.

"I don't know. Get some booze and go to the park."

Marco shuddered thinking about it. And now this Joe was heading his way with two other guys.

"This is Marco," Joe said when the coach left. "He's Italian. Lives in a huge house in Atherton, with a pool and a tennis court."

How did he know that?

"When are you gonna have a party, dude?"

"I'm not sure. I'll let you know." Actually his aunt and uncle said it was okay to throw a party for Marco's new friends. Even if his aunt and uncle weren't there, which they hardly ever were. They traveled a lot on business.

When he said he didn't have any friends, they laughed indulgently and said having a party was the way to get some. They were probably right.

First he'd invite those girls at that table back there who were now all waving to him. That was the way to start. Not that any one of them had anything to wear to a party. No fashion sense at all. He wondered if he'd see anyone wearing any decent clothes while he was in California.

One thing they didn't have in Italy was women with red hair like the girl he'd seen that morning standing in front of the school with the sun shining on her. Amazing color, like the sunset over the Adriatic.

The clarinet girl had made him think about music. His father had disapproved of Marco playing the piano. It reminded him of Marco's mother. But if he played at school this year his father wouldn't need to know. Yes, he was there to learn English and play soccer for the school. But life was more than learning those bewildering verbs and unpredictable prepositions and kicking a ball down the field, wasn't it? His mother had thought so.

He scanned the room across an acre of denim, looking for one single sign of style. Nothing. *Niente.*

eight

There was a young girl from Trinity
Who solved the square root of infinity.
While counting the digits,
She was seized by the fidgits
Dropped math and took up divinity.

—Author unknown

Cindy was surprised that the Italian had sat down at their table. After all, he was new and he didn't know those girls waving at him even though they were falling out of their chairs to catch his attention. He must have all the confidence of Italian royalty because he pulled out a chair, set his tray down and sat in the middle of the girls at the far end of the table. He never even glanced her way. Either he was avoiding her or he didn't remember her from this morning. Or both. No surprise there. She was used to being avoided and forgotten by guys.

She tried to pretend he wasn't there by nibbling at her salad and talking to Victoria or looking around the room, but all the time she was shamelessly listening to everything he said.

"So you play soccer," one of the girls said, bouncing up and down in eager excitement. Subtle she wasn't.

"Yes, a little. It's a good game."

"So where are you from?"

"Italy."

"Wow. That's so cool."

"Not this time of year. It's rather warm."

The girls laughed appreciatively and then all volunteered to give him lessons in American slang.

He very charmingly declined, finished his lunch and said *"Addio."* And still never noticed Cindy.

She didn't care. She didn't expect to be noticed. The really surprising thing was that he'd stopped by her locker this morning, picked up her clarinet and spoken to her at all. After all, she was taller than most guys (but not him), she had flaming red hair and a pale freckled face, and she had no clue how to flirt.

Besides, she was going to Manderley for the academics, not to hook up with guys—which she didn't know how to do—and not to make new friends, because she never would find any to match those she'd left behind. She was there to learn something! Yes, she knew how nerdy that sounded, so she kept it to herself. Herself and her friends that she'd left behind at Castle. And now she was on her way to AP geometry.

She pictured pages of triangles, quadratic equations and challenging problems that had solutions, like which sides of a polygon equaled the other sides. Problems unlike her lack of money and parents. Those were problems that were totally unsolvable. At least for now.

Geometry was held on the second floor of Manderley Hall, the beautifully restored old mansion that was the face of the school. Cindy tiptoed reverently across the faded Oriental carpets and climbed the wide curved staircase to room 117. It was a small class with maybe twelve or fifteen kids. Yes, this was what she'd come to Manderley for. A small math class with a teacher who had time to teach instead of yelling at the kids in the back row. Time to share his or her love of math with Cindy. But these kids wore signs of boredom etched on their faces. The kind of boredom of people who'd already had too many classes together. A few even looked up when she walked in. But no greetings. Not a smile. No "Welcome to our school."

She sat down in the second row. Five awkward, silent minutes passed.

"Five-minute rule," said a guy in the front row as he jumped up and put his books into his backpack.

"It's ten minutes, idiot," said another guy in the back row.

But before there could be a stampede for the door, a tall, thin woman in a long dress, canvas shoes and ropes of beads like some hippie out of the long-ago sixties came through the door.

"Sorry I'm late," she said. "But I just got the call. As you may know, I'm NOT your real teacher." She paused to give them a chance to react. But no one did. She cleared her throat. "I'm your substitute, Ms. Borrell. You can call me Anastasia."

More silence.

"Well, I've got your schedule and we're going to follow it just as if your regular teacher were here with you instead of me."

Call-me-Anastasia the substitute teacher stood in front of the chalkboard and closed her eyes. What did it mean? Cindy wondered. She turned around hoping to get clarification from someone. The guy sitting behind her who wore an amused expression and a gold hoop in each ear rolled his eyes and grinned at her.

Anastasia proceeded to exhale out of her mouth at the same time as she raised her open palms to the class. After a few more seconds of silence she slowly opened her eyes and smiled serenely at the students.

"I just need to get into a positive head space before I begin." She sat down on a stool and faced them. "So how is everyone today?"

Cindy murmured "fine," but her voice sounded weak and lonely.

"The first day of class is always so crazy," the teacher said sympathetically.

"Not as crazy as you are," someone muttered.

Cindy grimaced. She hoped the poor woman hadn't heard.

"I'm picking up some negative energy," Anastasia said with a wave of her heavily ringed hand. "And I'm guessing it has something to do with the subject matter. So here's what we're going to do. Something that works for me. Everyone take out a sheet of paper and write down all your negative thoughts."

No one moved. Everyone including Cindy stared at Anastasia as if she'd stumbled into their class from an alien universe. Apparently Cindy wasn't the only one who thought this was weird behavior from a teacher. Nevertheless Cindy took out a piece of paper. One by one the others did too.

"Go ahead," Anastasia said. "Start writing. We can't start class until you get rid of those bad thoughts. Every one of them. It doesn't have to be good grammar. Write fast. Write whatever bad vibe that comes into your head. Don't worry, I'm not going to collect them. I'm not even going to look at them. I'm going to show you how to get rid of everything that's weighing you down. Studying is okay. But first things first. What I'm going to teach you is how to dump your negativity. This is a really useful technique you can use the rest of your lives. Believe me, you'll thank me some day."

Okay, maybe this wasn't the strangest thing that had ever happened to Cindy, but yeah, sure, she had some negative thoughts she'd like to get rid of. Maybe Anastasia was right.

"Free association. Stream of consciousness. Just do it," Anastasia said as she walked around the room looking over their shoulders as they wrote.

Cindy wrote as fast as she could. She wrote about money and siblings and school and clothes and guys. When she finished, she did feel better. Almost as if she'd confided in a good friend. Like Lizzie. When it felt like she was alone in the world, she reminded herself her best friend was only a phone call away.

The sub was back in front of the class. "Now, crumple your papers and throw them at the chalkboard. Come on. Everybody. Let's see those balls of paper fly. One, two, three . . . heave!"

The crumpled papers started to fly so fast and furiously that Anastasia had to duck. Cindy's landed in the wastebasket.

"Good shot, Carrottop," a guy said.

She flushed. No one had called her Carrottop since she was five years old. It didn't bother her. Not much.

At that moment the door opened and a tall, ramrod-stiff man with a short buzz cut looked in.

"What in God's name are you doing here?" he asked Anastasia. "This is not Introduction to Psychology. This is geometry."

Anastasia's eyes widened. She muttered some obscenity, grabbed her shoulder bag and almost knocked the man over on her way out the door.

"This is inexcusable and it won't happen again, class," he said turning his head to watch Anastasia's hasty departure. "You're dismissed for today." He seemed to click his heels together before he left the room.

While everyone else filed out, Cindy just sat there, feeling slightly stunned. So this was Manderley. But it wasn't geometry. Who was that woman really? And who was the man?

Cindy finally stood up and found she wasn't the only one left. The guy behind her was still there.

"Just so you know, your hair is gorgeous," he said. "Not at all the color of carrots."

"You don't have to say that. It doesn't bother me," she said, wondering if everyone had heard the carrottop remark. "I've heard worse."

"I'm Scott," he said, "and I don't want to get all *Queer Eye* on you, but I'm wondering who does your hair."

"I'm Cindy and I do my hair myself."

"I'd love to get my hands on it," he said, squinting at her as if she were an abstract painting he was analyzing. "I'm just an amateur but I'm pretty good. It needs to be tamed. It needs layering. And some serious shaping. What do you say?"

"I . . . I don't know what to say. I'm not really into hair or clothes."

He nodded soberly. "I noticed. That's a mistake. You're new, aren't you?"

"Uh-huh."

"Heard you might be interested in joining the Gay-Lesbian Alliance."

"Don't you have to be gay?"

"Most of us are. I thought . . . I mean I heard from McHenry who heard from Bo who heard from your sister . . ."

Cindy's eyes widened. "My sister said I'm a lesbian?" she asked. Her face flamed. She felt like she'd just touched a live wire. That's how much it shocked her to think her sisters would spread a rumor about her. She'd kill Lauren or Brie or both of them. Why would they say that? What right did they have . . . "Not that there's anything wrong with it," she added, worried she might hurt his feelings. "It's just that . . ."

"My mistake," he said. "I still want to do your hair. Think about it. You can tell me tomorrow. *If* Nelson decides to show up. I had her last year and she's good—when she makes it to class, that is. Even if you're not gay, maybe you and I can study together. I'm pretty good at hair but I'm really good at math."

"Okay."

Cindy didn't know what else to say. Her sister had been spreading rumors that she was a lesbian, and how can a person stop a rumor like that? Someone else just offered to do a makeover for her, which she probably really needed. And maybe even offered to be her new friend, which she definitely needed. And this was just her first day.

Only two things were for sure. She was not a lesbian and she was definitely not bored.

nine

If your whole day is rotten, once they start the music, it seems to melt away.

—Donald O'Connor

Cindy stood in the open doorway of the band room for a long moment before she had the nerve to go in. Inside there was chaos. Kids yelling, goofing off, playing their instruments loudly and tunelessly or just staring off into space. Who was in charge? Apparently no one. Just when she was prepared to beg and plead for a chance to play with them. She had an audition piece ready. But who wanted to hear it?

The Italian prince was not there. If he really was a prince. That could just be a rumor along with everything else she'd heard about him. Yes, he looked like a prince, but maybe that's how all Italian guys looked. How would she know?

Maybe he was still looking for the band room. She hadn't seen him since lunch when he'd walked away from her table without even a glance at her. Not that it bothered her. She barely even thought about it at all.

She took a deep breath and walked into the music room. Nothing happened. No one noticed. Except for Scott from math class, who was standing in the corner next to a bass. He waved to her. She smiled and looked around to see if she knew anyone else.

There were about twenty kids, most of them making up a bloated rhythm section that featured at least four guitars. There was one other girl, a very large girl in a tight sweater who looked supremely confident. She might be the singer since she didn't appear to have an instrument. Or maybe someone's girlfriend?

Cindy's shoulders slumped. She'd expected more from the Manderley jazz band. Face it, she'd expected more from Manderley. What if she was paying $28,000 a year for this? A whacked-out substitute geometry teacher, a lackluster history class, mediocre students, spoiled rotten rich kids, an overly healthy and unsatisfying lunch, and now the chaos known as jazz band.

A short, stocky man with longish hair sauntered in. He had to be George Henderson, the bandleader. He looked overworked and haggard even though school had only just started. Maybe he'd get even more haggard as the year went on.

"Guys," Henderson said, taking the podium and placing his

hands on his hips. "Settle down." He took a folder out of his briefcase and read off the names. When he came to Cindy's name he looked up.

"Everyone, this is Cindy. New this year. Looks like she's got a clarinet there. Maybe we can play some traditional jazz this year for a change, even some swing. Unless the new head doesn't like jazz. Who knows?"

A few people in the bloated string section groaned softly. Cindy didn't look to see who they were. She didn't know if they were objecting to trad jazz or the new headmaster or both.

"Okay," he said, and continued to take roll.

"Harry Abrams."

"Yeah."

"Dylan Byrnes."

"Yo."

"Brad O'Connell."

"Here."

"Eric Shane." He paused. He looked at the empty piano bench next to Cindy. "Where's Eric?"

"I saw him talking to Michelle out there," a chubby trumpet player in a Berklee College of Music T-shirt said, pointing toward the quad.

"There he is," a long-haired guitar player said as he nodded his head toward the window. Henderson went to the wall of windows and was followed by the entire band. Cindy left her clarinet on a chair and went with them.

Scott came up behind her and whispered in her ear. "Probably asking her to the Welcome Dance. But she's way out of his league." He shook his head. "That's Eric. In the face of failure he's got this idiotic determination to persevere. If you stick around you'll see what I mean. And you should stick around. We need a good clarinet."

"I'm definitely sticking around," Cindy said. "And I've got determination too, idiotic or not. You didn't tell me you play the bass."

"You didn't ask," Scott said.

Henderson knocked on the window, his face red with anger. "*Eric,*" he yelled.

Eric turned around with shock on his face to see the entire band staring at him from the window, looked at his watch, appeared to say a quick good-bye to Michelle, then ran across the grass, dropping his music on the way. Henderson covered his face with his hands. Within minutes Eric crashed through the door to the band room.

"Sorry, Mr. Henderson," he said.

"Everyone, back to your places," Henderson said. "Take out 'Autumn Leaves.' You do remember 'Autumn Leaves' from last year, don't you?" His voice dripped with sarcasm. He obviously hated the song and thought it was beneath him. Cindy didn't blame him. "We need to work on it if we're playing it for Spirit Week. All right, let's start from the coda. Trumpets, let me hear you loudly on this one. We need to make sure the rhythm is very staccato . . . Eric, what are you doing?"

"Looking for my music," Eric said as he slid the piano bench forward.

"Do you even know the song?" one of the trumpeters asked under his breath. The whole trumpet section, who obviously hated poor Eric, laughed hysterically.

"Shut up, you guys, I can play it better than any of you," Eric said.

Once again Scott clued Cindy in. "He thinks he's the best piano player—hell, the best musician—in the whole school, if not the county."

"Dude, Michelle isn't gonna go to the dance with you, Eric," a trumpeter said sotto voce. "Get over it and stop asking her."

"*Guys!* Please, pleeeeease, be quiet. I'm serious, I cannot deal with this today." Henderson, for perhaps the hundredth or thousandth time since he'd been the bandleader, was obviously near the end of his rope. And it was just the first day of school. Cindy couldn't help feeling sorry for him.

Again Scott leaned forward to explain the situation. "Henderson's wife left him this summer for some Silicon Valley CEO. Everyone knows."

"That's terrible," Cindy said. No wonder the man looked so awful.

"Can't blame her. Ever try to live on a teacher's salary?"

No, but she was trying to live on the salary of a spa salon

assistant. She only hoped no one would guess how poor she really was. Her stepsisters wouldn't tell. Or would they? They seemed determined to sabotage her reputation at Manderley even before the first day had ended. It couldn't end fast enough for her.

Cindy might have fallen asleep during "Autumn Leaves" if it hadn't been for the Italian prince walking into the room. Henderson looked up. Cindy's mouth fell open. The guitars stopped playing. The trumpeters wiped the saliva from their mouthpieces. The room fell silent. It wasn't just the clothes—it was him. He had a presence. Probably not unusual for royalty.

"*Scusi*," he said. "I am Marco from Italy. This is the band, yes?"

"No," mumbled the guitar player. "It's Karate Club. How dumb can you be?"

"What can we do for you, Marco?" Henderson asked, ignoring the guitar section. The bandleader looked like he might bow down in front of Marco and kiss his ring.

"I play the piano. Not very well, but if you have a small part for me . . . ?" He raised his shoulders in a kind of Gallic shrug. Or it would have been Gallic if he'd been French. But he wasn't. He was Italian.

"Come on in," Henderson said, a faint smile on his tired face. "Are you familiar with 'Autumn Leaves'?"

ten

In Italian, a belladonna is a beautiful lady; in English, it's a deadly poison.

—Ambrose Bierce

While walking out to the parking lot with "Autumn Leaves" running through her head, Cindy got a message on her cell. It was from Brie telling her something had come up and they'd be late picking her up. She knew Irina would be mad if she was late to the salon, but Cindy hated to think of taking the bus with her clarinet and her heavy backpack. If only she were at Castle, any number of kids would have stopped and given her a ride. Here the cars whizzed by and passed her without a glance. After many long moments of sitting crosslegged on a patch of grass while she tried to read her history textbook, she looked up to see the Alfa cruising by.

Marco slowed and waved. Her breath caught in her throat. Her heart pounded. She turned around. No one there but her. He was waving at her. He had to be. Again. It wasn't possible, but it was happening. She stood and waved back. He kept driving. She started to walk slowly toward the car, not daring to hope he was waiting for her.

He kept driving and she kept walking until he stopped twenty-five yards away where two blond girls shrieked and piled into his car. Cindy stopped dead in her tracks. She stared in disbelief.

The blond girls waved to her. She could see the familiar smirks on their faces. She couldn't hear what they were saying but she could imagine . . .

"You don't think Marco was waving at you, do you, you pathetic loser? If you only knew how stupid you look, standing out there flapping your arm. You thought an Italian prince would be waving at you? Get real and go away, back where you belong. We told you you wouldn't make it at Manderley and you won't. Give up."

eleven

The word "good" has many meanings. For example, if a man were to shoot his grandmother at a range of five hundred yards, I'd call him a good shot, but not necessarily a good man.

—G. K. Chesterton

Marco was standing at the side of the field watching the most abysmal display of soccer playing he'd ever seen in his life when he got a call on his cell phone from his father.

"Do you know where your *nonna* is?" his father asked.

"No, why, is she lost?" Marco asked hopefully. He couldn't imagine his tiny little grandmother clad in black from head to toe getting lost on her way to mass, which was the only place she ever went anymore. But then maybe she'd been kidnapped. He could only hope, because this was the woman who had made his life miserable since he was five years old, when his parents got divorced and he was put under her care for his religious and spiritual education.

55

"She's on her way to Rome to catch a plane to come and see you."

"What?" Marco almost swallowed the whistle he was using to referee the game between the two varsity squads.

"Ever since you left she's been worried about you. Afraid you weren't getting enough to eat or weren't going to mass every day. You know she never wanted you to go to America. Then she saw something on television, some American program translated into Italian. *The Sopranos* I think it was. She couldn't sleep she was so worried."

"But that's about Italians. She's worried about Italians?"

"Italian-Americans. They're different. Worse. She thinks Italians turn bad when they reach the U.S. She's afraid that will happen to you."

"That's in New Jersey. I'm in California. There's no Mafia here. It's not like I'm alone. I have Aunt Cecilia and Uncle Leo."

"She tried calling them but they didn't answer. She got their answering machine. That's when she really got upset."

"*L'Oh, il mio dio*. You've got to stop her. She won't be happy here. No one speaks Italian."

"You do. You speak Italian. So do your aunt and uncle."

"Yeah, but they're never around."

"*No importa*. It's you she wants to see. Don't worry about her being happy. She's not happy anywhere. And it's too late to stop her," his father said cheerfully. Of course he was cheerful. He'd gotten rid of his interfering mother. "She's on her way."

"You could have told me before," Marco said, his jaw clenched tightly. He could have moved. Checked into a hotel. Faked his own death. Something. Anything. Maybe it wasn't too late.

"She wants to surprise you. Don't tell her I called you. And act surprised."

"I am surprised." Surprised and dismayed. Now what? The old lady was going to ruin his life. Pry into everything he was doing, from bagging girls to gambling. "I'm surprised you let her go. Isn't she kind of old for a trip like this?"

"Let her go? You try stopping her when she makes up her mind to do something."

Marco blew his whistle as a player on Team B fouled a player on Team A.

"She doesn't speak a word of English, does she?" Marco asked glumly.

"No, but she has a way of making herself understood," his father said.

Nonna made herself understood by pounding her cane on the floor or taking to her bed and telling everyone she was dying. That was the kind of language everyone understood.

Marco said good-bye, signaled, ran out onto the field and slammed the ball into the penalty area. The penalty area. Just where he'd be when his nonna got there. *Il dio lo aiuta!* God help him!

twelve

*Love and understand the Italians, for the people are more
marvelous than the land.*

—E. M. Forster

Two days passed before Cindy could look at herself in the mirror without blushing the color of her red hair. That's how em-
barrassed she was to think she'd made a fool of herself chasing
after Marco and his car. Not once but twice in the same day
had she imagined he was waving at her.

He was not just any Italian—he was a prince. On the other
hand, if there was ever a guy worth chasing, it was Marco.

It didn't help her get over her embarrassment when her sisters started in on her.

"If you only knew how ridiculous you looked running
after Marco in the parking lot. Can't you imagine what he

thinks about American girls? How desperate they are?" Brie said.

"We said we didn't know you," Lauren said. "What were you thinking?"

There was no answer to that, so Cindy said nothing. Which only seemed to encourage them.

"You think it's easy having a loser of a sister show up at your school like this? You think we like being connected to you in any way?" Brie demanded. "We told you not to tell anyone we're related, which we aren't, but somehow the word is out. We've spent three years waiting for our senior year and you're ruining it for us. Do you even know what people are saying about you? I think you like making our lives miserable."

Cindy pressed her lips together to keep from telling them she'd *love* to make their lives miserable. And if she really wanted to, she could think of a dozen ways to do it. But she was too nice. Too nice to say anything. Too nice to tell them that she knew what people were saying about her and that she knew who was saying it: It was *them*. She *was* too damn nice.

After they finished with Cindy, they switched to their favorite subject.

"He's a real honest-to-God prince," Brie informed her sister.

"I know that," Lauren said. "Everyone knows that. He's got a castle in Tuscany."

"And a country house in Bellagio next door to George Clooney's on the lake where they filmed *Ocean's Twelve*.

"And he had a part in the film."

"No way!"

"Way!"

"We've got to watch that movie again."

The consensus was that not only was Marco rich and titled, he was also a champion soccer player and totally gorgeous, which was obvious to anyone with 20-40 vision.

Every day on the way to and from school Brie and Lauren competed with each other to see who could top the latest Marco story or who had the inside track with him.

Stuck once again in the backseat of the Cherokee, Cindy was subjected to their ravings. At least they'd stopped trashing her for a few days.

If she'd had a wool hat she would have pulled it over her ears and tuned them out, but the usual September temperatures were in the eighties.

Or, like an ordinary teenager, she could have turned up the volume on her iPod. Of course Cindy was not ordinary in any sense, and had no consumer electronic devices. She had an old Macintosh computer that her father left her with dial-up Internet connection. It was set up in the corner of her tiny closet that Irina had designated as her "office" when legal services had come to check on her status as a minor child under Irina's guardianship. If she really hated hearing them talk about how princely and sexy Marco was, Cindy could have tried meditation as a way of tuning their remarks out, but the fact was, she hung on every word and filed it away.

Even when the stories bordered on the scandalous.

"You know why he's here, don't you?" Brie said to Lauren in a hushed voice with a glance over her shoulder at Cindy. "Because he wants to go to an American university next year."

"That's just a rumor," Lauren said.

Cindy sat up straight and leaned forward. If she didn't take advantage of this opportunity she would hate herself later. "Speaking of rumors," she said lightly, "did either of you hear that I'm supposed to be gay?"

The girls laughed.

"No, really?" Brie said. "Are you?"

"No," Cindy said.

"It's a logical assumption," Lauren said as if she even knew what logic was. "You've never had a boyfriend. How were we supposed to know? Besides, who cares anyway? It's cool if you're gay or bi or transsexual or whatever at Manderley. So if you're thinking of a sex change operation . . . go for it." This was enough to send them into gales of uproarious laughter.

"I'm not," Cindy said glaring at the back of their heads. So it was true. They really were spreading rumors about her. She blinked back angry tears. What could she do? Go around telling people she wasn't gay? Her sisters had been there for three years. They had friends and she didn't. Who would listen to her? Who would believe her? Who would care what she was?

After they'd recovered from that burst of hilarity, then went back to the subject of Marco.

"The real reason Marco's here," Lauren said to her sister, "is that his family is in the Mafia, his father is the godfather, and there's a price on his head, so they sent him here to escape being killed by a rival family."

"Oh my God, then if the bad guys find out he's here, we could all be in danger."

"I don't care. I'd protect him. We could hide him at our house."

"What I heard was that he got some girl pregnant back in Italy and he didn't want to marry her, so he left without telling his family and they don't even know where he is."

With these rumors ringing in her ears, Cindy was dropped off at the spa after school every day. She decided that reacting to their scummy gossip about her was just what they wanted, so she forced herself to stay cool and pretend she didn't care what they said. As for the gossip about Marco, she didn't know what to believe and she couldn't ask him.

Unfortunately the warm weather didn't keep women from tanning themselves artificially or subjecting themselves to exfoliations or rich chocolate scrubs. So Cindy had to fold towels, sweep the floor, answer the phones and make appointments for sunless fake tans and Swedish massages.

One thing she didn't do, to Irina's disgust, was pressure any clients to sign up for a weekly package of spray-on tan plus mud wrap. Nor did she push the sale of insta-tan towelettes for touch-ups at home. Irina pursed her gel-augmented lips and told Cindy she was a failure as a salesperson. Cindy tried to look apologetic as she nodded in agreement.

The next Friday she got a break. Instead of heading for the salon after school, she was on her way to the library to tutor a student when her cell phone rang.

"Where are you?" Irina asked. "I have three clients here for spray-on tans and one for a hand and foot reflexology."

"I told you I couldn't come in today," Cindy said patiently. "I have work-study."

"What's that?"

"It's part of my scholarship. Some days I work in the office during my free period. Today I tutor."

"Forget work-study. There's work and there's study. This is work. Real work. It's about time you learned the difference. I can't run this salon by myself." She didn't say she was too cheap to hire decent help when she could get Cindy to work for minimum wage.

Cindy could just picture Irina frowning, though it was hard to tell when no lines appeared on her smooth Botoxed forehead.

"Maybe Brie or Lauren . . ." Cindy suggested.

"They have cheerleading after school. You know that. Cheerleaders are getting good scholarships these days. Because it's an actual sport. You can't just be beautiful anymore. You have to be athletic too. Cheerleading incorporates dance, tumbling, you name it."

Cindy was tempted to name it something else, but she kept her mouth shut and Irina went on.

"I have to think of their future. I'm just lucky they're so talented. And beautiful. And hardworking. Two girls in college at the same time. That's some expense. Think about it. It's not going to be easy for me even if they get the scholarships they deserve."

As if she hadn't inherited all of Cindy's father's money. Just when Cindy was sure Irina never gave a thought to her own future, Irina showed she did give her a thought. "You could have a future here, you know."

"Here?" Cindy was so shocked she almost dropped her bag. "Where?"

"At the salon. You're good at math. You're not very good at sales or service, but you could keep the books for me."

"I'll think about it," Cindy said. She'd rather haul king crab from the frigid Bering Sea onto a sinking trawler in an ice storm than work for her stepmother after high school. She had other plans for the rest of her life that didn't include her stepfamily.

"Remember, there's no money for you for college, but you could take some classes in massage therapy at the community college if you want to improve yourself."

Cindy bit her tongue to keep from retorting, "Just what I've always wanted, a career pounding the backs of rich, vain women." She knew Irina could spend her father's money any way she liked. She certainly didn't like spending an extra penny on Cindy. And, legally, she didn't have to, as long as she kept a roof over her head and food on the table. Cindy managed to say a noncommittal "Uh-huh" before she hung up.

Cindy loved the library. Instead of the smell of grape washes and seaweed enzymes, there was the smell of new books and new carpets and a view of the grassy fields and the classic buildings from the huge floor-to-ceiling windows of the state-of-the-art, one-year-old, T. J. Ransom Memorial Library.

She set her backpack on a table in the corner. She had no idea who the academically challenged person she was supposed to tutor was. Probably some dumb jock. Or a freshman who wasn't used to Manderley's high standards and demanding assignments. Or a senior who was in danger of not getting into the college of his choice unless he passed English. It didn't matter. The school office knew what she was good at and would never assign her to help someone in, say, advanced Latin, for example. She'd tutored at Castle last year and she knew it was satisfying to get someone to make progress in a subject they sucked at. *If* they cared. *If* they were willing to try. Even if they weren't, anything was better than working at the salon.

This quiet corner of the library had been set aside for individual help sessions. She was early so she took her notebook out and started working on her geometry homework.

A few moments later, when she was in the middle of the extra credit question, she heard footsteps.

"Uh, Cindy?"

She looked up. Oh, no, the one person she didn't want to see. Was she going to have to tutor her slacker history partner who'd already stood her up for their meeting after class to discuss the paper, in addition to doing the whole paper by herself?

thirteen

I think war might be God's way of teaching us geography.

—Paul Rodriguez

"Hi, Toby, are you looking for me?" *Please say you aren't.*

"Not really, but I saw you and I was wondering . . ."

Whew. He was not here to get tutored. It was bad enough she had to do this report with him. *For* him, was more like it.

"About our report?"

"Yeah, we're supposed to be doing something, aren't we?" he asked vaguely.

Just as Cindy feared, Toby didn't have a clue.

"We have an outline due on Monday." She reached into her backpack, pulled it out and handed it to him. "I hope you don't mind I did it without you, but you haven't been in class and you blew off our meeting so I called you and left a message. I wanted to know what part of the war you thought we should concentrate on."

"Sorry, I haven't been checking my messages. I've had a few problems."

She nodded. Didn't everyone have problems? Even her stepsisters were having problems deciding what to wear to the Welcome Dance next weekend. She had no idea what Toby's problems were and she really didn't want to find out.

"Wow, this looks great." He sounded surprised. "Says here our report's gonna be on the Pacific. So who was fighting out there?"

"America and Japan, mostly. I didn't think we could do the whole war, so I picked a few battles."

Toby nodded. "Leyte. Corregidor." He stumbled over the pronunciation. "Wherever that is. I've heard of them. Somewhere. Somebody. I know, it's my grandfather. He was there."

"There? Where? In the war you mean?"

"Yeah. He's got all these medals and stuff."

"Really? Is he still alive?"

"Pretty much, but he's not doing too well. He lives at Lily Langtry Gardens in Palo Alto with all the other old people. He hates it there. He hates old people."

"But . . ."

"I know, he's old too, but he's kind of out of it, you know?"

"So out of it, he couldn't come and talk to the class about

the war? That would be so cool if he could. Better than a PowerPoint presentation. More interesting. More personal."

"I don't know. I could ask him. He's still got his uniform."

"No kidding?" Cindy could see it now. An old man, a proud veteran in his uniform with his medals, sharing his memories with a class of smart-ass kids who needed to be shaken out of their complacent lives by someone from the Greatest Generation. Kids who might think history was irrelevant. It might be a way to impress their teacher too. She knew how important it was to score points at the beginning of the semester, in case something came up and she had to slack off at some point later. At least that's what always worked at Castle. "Would he wear it?"

Toby shrugged. "I guess."

Cindy snatched the outline back from Toby. "Can you find out exactly where he was in the war and when it was? I'll redo the outline. This could be really good."

"Good enough to get a B on this? I could use a good grade in something."

"A B? I plan on getting an A."

"An A in history?" He sounded incredulous.

"An A in everything." Cindy could have bitten her tongue. What made her brag like that?

Toby's eyes opened a little wider than his usual half-mast. "An A would be good. An A would be awesome. I'll go see him. Some days he's out of it. Some days he's full of himself. Maybe we'll get lucky."

Toby gave her a lopsided smile. Maybe he wasn't really stupid, he just looked that way. At least she had his attention.

"Whatever happens, let me know," Cindy said firmly. "We have to decide what we're doing this weekend."

He nodded, backed away and knocked over a tall stack of books on his way out. Cindy started to get up to help him pick them up, but the librarian suddenly appeared out of nowhere and told Toby to pretty much get the hell out of there before he did any more damage and let a professional put the shelf back up again.

fourteen

You can't prevent the birds of sorrow from flying over your head, but you can prevent them from building nests in your hair.

—Chinese proverb

Once Toby was out of sight, Cindy went back to the extra-credit geometry problem the real teacher, Mr. Nelson, had assigned. She and Scott, her new friend from geometry, had a competition going to see who could solve it first. She'd seen Scott in the far corner of the library on her way in. He was listening to music on his iPod and had an intense look on his face.

She was just drawing triangles on her paper when Scott leaned over her shoulder.

She jumped. "You scared me."

"Sorry, what's that?" he said, pointing to her paper.

"*That* is going to be the answer to the problem," she said, flipping the page over. "Don't tell me you haven't solved it yet."

Instead of answering, he took the seat next to her. "Did you find AB and CD?"

"I think so. By using the Pythagorean theorem."

"Me too," he said. "But how are you going to find EF?"

"Wouldn't you like to know?"

"Hah, I already know. I just worked it out."

"Show me."

"Not till you admit I won our bet. You owe me."

A soft voice broke into their conversation. "Hi, Cindy."

It was Victoria, her other new friend who she'd been eating with every noon since that first day. "Victoria, this is Scott. He's in my geometry class."

"AP geometry? You must be smart," Victoria said with a sigh. "I can barely balance my checkbook."

"I am," Scott said with a grin. "Okay, I'll leave you gossip girls. Cindy, I'll collect tomorrow."

"What did he mean?" Victoria asked.

"We had a bet on who could do the extra-credit problem first." She flipped her paper over. "It's hard. Look at it. If he won, I have to bring brownies to the Gay-Lesbian Alliance meeting next week. And no, I'm not gay, but anyone can go to the meetings. Sit down. You're not here to get tutored, are you?" Cindy asked.

"No, I'm tutoring somebody in Chinese. Have you seen him?"

"I haven't seen anyone. I'm waiting for someone too. Someone who needs help in English, I hope."

"How will we know? Why don't we have their names?" Victoria said with a tiny frown on her perfect oval face.

"When I checked with the office, they were overwhelmed," Cindy said. "They had too many kids asking for tutors. I just hope whoever they are got the message and they'll be here. Otherwise, I should be at work."

"I wanted to tell you I just paid my parking tickets."

"Good for you. I hope it wasn't too expensive."

"It doesn't matter. I just ask my parents for more money. They can afford it." If anyone else had said that, Cindy would have been put off, but Victoria was so matter-of-fact about being rich, Cindy couldn't be offended.

"They keep me busy. I handle their bank account here, which isn't easy since I'm so terrible at math, along with the mortgage payments and the other bills. It's a big job, considering I've got so much homework to do. No one told me Manderley was going to be so hard." She rubbed her forehead with her palm as if to make sure no facts came leaking out before she had a chance to use them in class.

"You could go to Castle. Believe me, you'd have a four point without any effort," Cindy suggested.

"But would I get into an Ivy League school or Berkeley? Isn't that the point of a Manderley education?"

"It is for me," Cindy said. "So after you get your prestigious BA degree, then what? Back to Hong Kong?"

"I don't know. Sometimes I wonder where I belong. I don't really feel at home here or there. My father is more Chinese than my mother, even though he's from Fresno, if you can believe that. They have this house, but whether they'll ever live in it is another matter. My mother says no. You know that Ella Fitzgerald song, 'The Lady Is a Tramp'? ' . . . hates California, it's cold and it's damp.' " That's my mom. But she wants me to go to Berkeley or Harvard or Princeton. It would give her something to brag to her friends about. Sometimes I envy you, Cindy. You don't have to live up to anyone's expectations."

"Except my own," Cindy murmured. She didn't say those same schools were where she wanted to go too, but what if Victoria didn't take her seriously? What if she thought, *How can you, Cindy, even dream such a dream without any money or support from your family?* No, it was best to keep such plans to herself for now.

Just then a tall, blond, tanned athletic guy came loping casually toward them with a big smile on his face. He looked upbeat, like he was looking forward to learning something and getting help. If this was the guy who was assigned to her, she'd never complain again.

He was obviously the kind of student every tutor wanted. Eager and enthusiastic. After tutoring for the past two years she had a pretty good idea of who would try and who wouldn't.

Besides looking like the caring type, he was cute too, in a certain all-American athletic way. The kind of guy her sisters would fall for.

Cindy pushed her chair back and gave him a welcoming smile. Just in case. She couldn't be that lucky, could she? No, she couldn't.

"Who's Victoria Lee?" he asked. "I need help with my Chinese."

fifteen

If you can speak three languages, you're trilingual.
If you can speak two languages, you're bilingual. If you
can speak only one language, you're an American.

—Author unknown

Victoria smiled warmly, said she'd be his tutor, and she and the guy, whose name was Steve, went to another table. Soon Cindy could hear him trying to pronounce the Chinese words Victoria said, which made her giggle helplessly and made him try even harder to make her laugh. The instant rapport they had filled Cindy with envy, an emotion she fought with every fiber of her being, day in and day out.

She tried to get back to her geometry problem but she kept glancing up and studying the two of them across the room. They made a really cute couple. Physically as well as mentally. Victoria could help him with his Chinese, and he could help her with her English. If she needed any help, which seemed unlikely. Cindy wondered if she'd ever make a cute couple with anyone or have instant rapport with a guy.

What a contrast they were. This tiny, dark-haired, lovely half-Chinese girl in her expensive American jean jacket, short skirt and wedge high heels and a big, blond super-confident all-American jock in cutoff shorts and a tight T-shirt that showed off his all-American muscles.

How would Cindy find someone to contrast with her tall, freckled self? He would have to be even taller, and not pale and anemic looking like she was. He'd have to have straight hair because hers was curly. He would have a big happy family because she had no one. It was hard to picture such a person.

It was even harder to get back to work with the image of the mysterious opposite in her head, even work that she liked. Before she could force herself to write a single equation, she heard footsteps on the carpet.

Her skin tingled and her senses went on alert, the way a person would feel if she got too close to the magnetic field of a nearby star, like maybe Betelgeuse. She raised her eyes and there he was. Her complete opposite. He was tall and olive-skinned. She was fair and freckled. He was rich. She was poor. He had a family, at least a godfather. She had no one.

This time he was wearing a striped jersey, black shorts and shoes with cleats. His hair was damp and his skin seemed to glow with a bronze that didn't come out of a spray can. The answer to every girl's dreams. Not just hers.

"*Ciao*," he said with a dazzling smile. "I'm looking for my English tutor. I hope it will be you, say yes."

Say yes? How could she say anything else? "Yes, it is," Cindy said as the heat rushed to her face. "I mean she's me . . . her."

sixteen

Marco pulled out a chair and sat next to Cindy. *Right* next to Cindy. So close she couldn't catch her breath. She wondered if the cooling system had failed. All the air was being sucked out of the building. Instead of the smell of books, there was the faint smell of citrus and Italian leather in the air.

With shaky fingers she pushed her geometry problem aside. But he'd seen the diagram.

"What is this?" he asked, leaning toward her so that his arm brushed against hers. His breath was warm on her neck.

"Nothing." Was that her voice, that breathy, scratchy sound? "A geometry problem. I have to find the area of the square."

He traced the outline of the square DEFG with one finger. "You're good at this? Yes, I think you are. Music and mathematics. They go together. In some people. Not me. Let me see how you do this problem."

"Now? It's going to take a while." A while for her to recover her brainpower. At the moment she'd have trouble solving Y plus X equals Z, even if they gave her the values of Y and X.

"See," she said, "the square DEFG is inside a right triangle, ABC. They give you AD and GC, but that's all. I can do it later. It's for extra credit."

"What means extra credit?"

"It means you don't have to do it. Only if you want to."

"You don't have to do it? Then why?"

"Why? Because I like to solve problems." *And get good grades.*

He shook his head. "I don't like problems. I came to U.S. to get away from problems. But some of them, one of them is following me here."

"Following you?" Maybe it was true what her sisters had said about Marco and his Mafia connections. She looked out the window half expecting to see a couple of Italian men in dark clothes walking toward the library. But all she saw were freshmen tossing a Frisbee back and forth on the grass. Was it really the Mafia he was talking about? Or was it his pregnant girlfriend? Was he going to tell her? Should she ask? Did she really want to know? Wouldn't she prefer to think of him as a fun-loving, easygoing Mediterranean without a care in the world?

"Never mind. This is not your worry." He reached over and smoothed the line on her forehead with his finger. Her vision blurred and her cheeks flamed. She told herself it was just a casual gesture and it meant nothing. But she blushed again anyway.

"Right now I need to think about my terrible English," he said, leaning back in his chair and balancing on the rear legs.

"It's not terrible," she assured him. "It's very good. Of course you have an accent. But you shouldn't lose it altogether. It's uh . . . nice." Nice? It was seductive, it was sexy and it wrapped around Cindy like a warm blanket and left her tingling all over.

"Nice? I don't think so," he said. "I wish I'd started English when I was a child, like you did." He cocked his head and studied her face as if he was trying to picture her as a child.

"I wish I could learn Italian," she said. "It's a beautiful language."

"Yes?" he said. "How do you know?"

"Oh, I uh . . ." Cindy couldn't possibly confess she'd checked out some Italian language tapes from the language lab and had already learned how to ask directions to the bus station and how to say she was sick and needed to find a doctor.

"You can learn Italian. It's easy," he said. "I can teach you."

"It's probably too late," she said. But her heart skipped a

beat. She pictured Marco teaching her love songs in Italian. Like the ones in the operas her father used to listen to late at night.

"Not for you. You're clever. And you are very kind. I knew this when first I see you at your locker. You have a kind face."

Cindy didn't want to have a kind face. She would have given anything to have a beautiful face, but that was not to be.

"Look," Marco said, pulling a book out of his backpack. "See what I have to do for my class—Rebels in American Literature. I think this sounds good, yes? So I enroll for this class. Because I love American rebels. Like James Dean, you know him? But then I get the books today for this class. Look." He leaned forward, opened a bag and spilled some books out on the table.

"*Huckelberry Finn. The Awakening. One Flew Over the Cuckoo's Nest.* How can I read all this in English? I don't even know what is a cuckoo."

"It's a bird. But there's another meaning. To be cuckoo means crazy."

"Ah, slang." He nodded happily. "This is what I need to know. What I can't learn in books. American slang. What is this thing called a mixer I hear about? Is it slang?"

"A mixer is a kind of dance party. Where they mix up the students." She made a mixing motion with her hands. "So they can get to know each other."

"I must attend this mixer?"

"Since you're new, I think it would be a good way to meet people."

"The same for you. You are new too. So you will also be there? Then I will know someone at least."

Like he didn't know anyone else? "What about the soccer team? You know them."

"Boys," he said dismissively. "I prefer girls."

Like the girl he left behind in Italy? The one who was pregnant?

"I . . . I'll be selling tickets at the door." That way she wouldn't have to pay the fifteen-dollar admission. And she wouldn't have to stand around alone looking like the outsider she was. She'd have a reason to be there. After she sold tickets she'd pour punch into paper cups and keep busy. Too busy to dance or talk to strangers.

Cindy looked at her watch. "Maybe we should work on what you need for your class first before we do any slang."

"Yes, yes. First thing is I must write about myself. Everyone must do this too. How I am a rebel. If I am a rebel. What do you think?"

She stole a glance at his profile, his angular jaw and his slightly crooked nose. A rebel with a soccer injury? A rebel who'd left a scandal behind in Italy? She told herself to calm down. To quit thinking of Marco as a gorgeous prince or a movie star and more like just another student who needed her help learning English. She could do it. She'd tutored foreign students at Castle. Helped them with their grammar, punctuation and spelling. None of them had looked like Marco of course. She'd had no trouble keeping her distance from them. No trouble forgetting about them after their sessions together.

"I don't know if you are or not," she said. "Let's see. We could make a list. What makes a rebel? How do you fit in?"

Cindy took out a sheet of notebook paper and drew a line down the middle—one side for the characteristics of a rebel, the other for characteristics of Marco Valenti. For the next hour they discussed Marco's personality, his friends in Italy, his family and his dream of driving a Porsche Spyder across America like his hero James Dean. Or an Italian Lancia.

At the end of the hour Marco had the first paragraph of his essay written in pretty much his own words, as well as an outline for the rest of the paper. At the end of the hour Cindy still didn't know if he really was a prince, if he'd been in the *Oceans Eleven* movie or if he had a girlfriend back in Italy.

But she knew more important things about him. She knew by reading between the lines that he had self-confidence, charm, kindness and honesty, and that she'd fallen head over heels in love with him. Or at least in lust, as her sisters would say. Not that it mattered. She would keep her infatuation to herself the way she kept everything else bottled up inside.

Cindy was also proud of Marco for his rapid progress in writing his paper in English, while never giving up his seductive accent. She was proud of herself for not correcting his English any more than she absolutely had to. It would be so easy to just rewrite the paper for him. But that was cheating. And the final product wouldn't sound like him.

She was not proud of herself for falling under his spell quite so fast and so easily. But who could resist that accent, his European manners, the occasional low chuckle when she said something he thought was funny, and the touch of his hand on her arm to punctuate his words.

Yes, she knew it was stupid and pointless to let herself get carried away like this. This was no ordinary guy. This was a foreign exchange student. Someone who'd be gone at the end of the school year, either returning to his country or going to college in the U.S., and she'd never see him again. Besides, she was not the kind of girl he would ever fall for.

"About this rebel idea," Marco said, leaning back in his chair so he was balancing on the rear two legs and surveying her with a curious gaze. "I'm not sure I understand. Tell me if you are one."

"Me, a rebel? Oh . . . I don't think so."

Marco opened his English dictionary and thumbed through the pages. "Here it is. Rebel. I should have looked it up before. But I like hearing you explain things to me. I'm very lazy, yes?"

A little smile tugged at the corner of her mouth.

"It says here," he said, " 'Rebel. Disobedient. Resists or defies authority.' This is not you, is it?" He narrowed his gaze and kept it focused on her.

"Oh, no. Sometimes I'd like to be a rebel, but I'm not. Not ever. I look up to people who stand up for themselves, like my father. He quit his job years ago to work for himself, and he rebelled against the system. Even though he knew independent inventors hardly ever make it on their own. Not many people quit a high-paying job to take a chance like that. He believed in himself. His wife, my stepmother, didn't. She told him he'd never make it. She told him to get a real job. So he had to rebel against her too. She was so angry he'd forced her to be the breadwinner." His puzzled expression caused her to stop and explain. "A breadwinner is the person who earns the money in the family, who brings home the bread."

"Ah," he said with a smile. "The bread is very important in Italy too. As well as the pasta. Perhaps you have nothing to rebel against."

"Maybe not," she said. But what about the pressure her sisters put on her and the lies they told about her? What about the job her stepmother made her do? Nothing worth rebelling against? "Anyway, I'm not the kind who'd rock the boat."

"What boat?" he asked with a puzzled look.

"It's just a saying. It means I don't want to upset the situation the way it is. I sit quietly in the boat because I don't want the boat to sink and me to drown. Does that make sense?"

He gave her a long look before he spoke. "So you always do what you're supposed to do. Like your homework."

"Yes, of course, but also, I work for my stepmother after school. She's my boss, both at home and at work. My stepsisters tell me what to do too."

"You have sisters? Do they look like you with the amazing red hair?"

Cindy laughed. "No, they're blond and beautiful. I think you know them, Brie and Lauren."

"Those girls are related to you?" He sounded incredulous.

"Not really. Sort of. My father married their mother."

"Ah, I see. So you don't rebel even though you would like to. I think you're a very good girl."

Was that a compliment or was he thinking, *You're a very good girl, but good girls are boring and besides, you're also a wimp of the first degree.*

When he left to play soccer a few minutes later, she put her head down on her loose-leaf binder and closed her eyes. She couldn't move. Couldn't speak. She was drained. It was exhausting trying to act casual and tutorial when she just wanted to sit there and stare at him, listen to him talk, giggle, flirt, repeat some Italian phrases and talk about herself.

She'd talked too much about herself. As for flirting and giggling, she didn't know how to do those things. Besides, it was not part of the job description of a tutor. She was there to help him with his English grammar. But she usually forgot to listen for grammatical errors when he talked. He could have read the phone book and she would have hung on every word he spoke in his seductive accent. Maybe working at the spa was easier than tutoring after all. Less stressful.

seventeen

1) For every action, there is an equal and opposite criticism.
2) Odd objects attract fire.

—Murphy's Laws of Combat, Anonymous

"My name is Newton Kavanaugh and I'm your new headmaster." The man stood on the stage in the middle of the Michael P. and Emily C. Parsons Multi-Use Room, folded his arms across his chest and rocked back on the heels of his spit-polished black shoes. He surveyed the student body with the manner of a man speaking to his troops. One who was accustomed to being in command. He was not wearing a uniform, but somehow he gave the impression he was. In fact, he was wearing well-pressed gray slacks, a striped shirt and a blue blazer with brass buttons.

"I'm a military man and proud of it. Always was, always will be. My father was a four-star general and I was an army brat. Of course I will never achieve his rank, and—ahem—at this point in my life, I have no need to. I served in Vietnam and retired with the rank of colonel. You can call me Colonel or Sir." He gave a faint smile.

Cindy realized he was the man who'd come into her math class that first day. It was hard to know if he was serious about calling him colonel. Cindy looked around. There was more shock than awe on the faces of the students.

From somewhere behind her a boy's voice muttered, "Oh jeez," but Kavanaugh showed no sign of having heard it.

To one side she saw Marco surrounded by members of the soccer team. At least she thought that's who they were. They all wore the same striped jerseys and the same blank looks on their faces. As if they'd spent too much time heading the ball instead of passing and kicking.

Cindy had learned a little about soccer. She'd read that studies showed there was no link between lower intelligence and a tendency to "head the ball," but observing the team members at Manderley, she wondered about it. Marco was excluded of course. He was smart, he was sexy and he was also suave and she was looking forward to their next tutoring session more than she should. She planned to surprise him with a few new phrases she'd learned in Italian, though at the last minute she'd probably lose her nerve. She didn't need to know Italian to help him perfect his English, which was already quite good.

She just wanted to be able to say something in that beautiful, romantic language.

Kavanaugh's gaze shifted from the students to the row of teachers seated in front of him.

"I was proud to represent my country," he continued, "just as I know you are proud to represent Manderley School. After my military service, I joined Cuthbert Military Academy as an instructor in military history, which is my hobby as well as my main academic interest." He paused to let this information sink in. Cindy felt a wave of restlessness in the assembled academic body, but maybe that was just her being overly sensitive.

"Eventually I became headmaster at Cuthbert for seven years until the board of directors here at Manderley convinced me I'd be the right man to whip this school into shape." He smiled briefly. "After what one of them called an 'era of laxity.' If you know what I mean."

At this, Cindy noticed several teachers in the front row looked at each other and there was a low rumble of voices from the students that sounded anxious, or possibly even angry, but which Kavanaugh seemed to interpret as approval. Maybe that's because it's all he'd ever heard in the military or at Cuthbert.

"My experience has shown over and over again that even in the best of institutions, which Manderley certainly is, without strong leadership and strict standards, discipline begins to falter."

Falter? What did that mean? Had it faltered last year? Before that? Being new to the school, Cindy really didn't know.

"Now there are those in modern society who say 'mature' people already have the sense and discipline to behave themselves. They think it's not our place to make rules such as a zero-tolerance drug and alcohol policy and a secure monitored campus. They think it's wrong to punish those who break our rules because it might put a damper on their children's precious creativity." Here his mouth twisted in a slight sneer and his cold eyes swept accusingly across the teachers in the front rows. His earlier friendly expression had hardened into a grimace that suggested his opinion of this view bordered on treason. And everyone knew what the punishment for treason was.

"We're at war, people," he said, gripping the podium, leaning forward and raising his voice. "At war against mediocrity, laziness, counterculture values, immorality and just plain slovenliness. I learned in the military what a powerful effect good discipline, structure and a certain rigidity has on performance and morale. At Cuthbert they worked just as well as they will work here. I have been given the challenge to institute some of these same changes at your school and I will do it.

"Change number one. Students will be evaluated not only on academics, which are important of course, but on cooperation, respect, hygiene and honesty."

Cindy looked around. Rebellious murmurs filled the air. Students were wide-eyed. Some teachers looked like they'd been hit with a cattle prod. With Kavanaugh in charge, it wasn't that far-fetched.

Kavanaugh seemed unaffected. "By earning points, students can improve their rank. I will post a complete list of rankings so the whole school knows who's above or below them—along with a list of ways to improve rankings, such as volunteering for honor guard, drill team and campus monitor." He looked around as if he expected to receive a standing ovation for his plan. He didn't. There was only a stunned silence. But that didn't stop him. He continued.

"Moving right along. Here's one of my most popular in-novations at Cuthbert. Calisthenics before school. As soon as I can hire some drill instructors we will have mandatory work-outs every morning at seven-thirty. No excuses. No absences. No exceptions. Even for our outstanding athletes. Now I have only one question for you. Are you willing to become a better school? Do you want to change? Are you with me?"

He waited for the thunderous applause that didn't come. There was only a smattering of polite clapping. In fact, the audience seemed to have fallen into a collective trance, totally puzzled as to how to react. Then he strode off the stage and took a seat. The student body president made some announce-ments about a change in the schedule and about the mixer coming up the next week.

With a nervous side glance at the new headmaster, the president told the students that there were new rules in place for the mixer, such as no student who'd been caught imbibing alcohol or wearing improper clothing or engaging in immoral behavior on the dance floor would be allowed to participate in the dance.

There was a moment of shocked silence before the kids started booing. The president quickly left the stage. The noise level skyrocketed as the students poured into the halls on their way back to class.

"What did you think?" Cindy's friend Scott asked when she saw him in the hall.

"I don't know," she said. "I've never met a headmaster before." She raised her eyebrows. "You look worried."

"Worried? The guy is psycho. Did you hear what he said? Do you know what it means? Calisthenics? A ranking system? What rank do you think you'd get?"

Cindy shook her head. "Private first class?"

"You wish. Because you're new you'd be a buck private. Nope, life at Manderley will never be the same. I'm calling a special meeting of the Gay-Lesbian Alliance today. This guy has got to be stopped. Care to join us?"

"But I'm not . . ."

"I know you're not gay. You don't have to be."

"I'm not a rebel either."

He squeezed her arm. "I know, but I like you anyway."

eighteen

The worse you are at thinking
the better you are at drinking.

—Terry Goodkind

Toby met Richard in the school parking lot on the night of the Welcome Dance. If it weren't for Richard's boring econo-Nissan Sentra his uptight parents (who'd surprisingly been friends of Toby's not-so-uptight parents since forever) thought was appropriate for an uptight kid his age, the parking lot could have doubled for a Lexus dealership. Most of Toby's friends were driving the most expensive cars on the market.

And why shouldn't they? Their fathers were CEOs or venture capitalists or entrepreneurs who courted venture capitalists. Some may have failed at their first attempt to become Silicon Valley millionaires, and were left with a portfolio of worthless stock options. But if they had any balls, they'd just picked up the pieces and started again. Until they'd finally succeeded.

Some were retired professional athletes whose kids were on the Manderley teams. If any of these parents couldn't afford a luxury car for their sons or daughters, well, the kids didn't have any business going to Manderley. At least that's what Toby thought.

Clearly nervous, Richard looked around the parking lot. "Where're Steve and Jared?" he asked. You'd think he'd never had a drink before a dance before. Maybe he hadn't. Come to think of it, he didn't remember seeing Richard at the dances last year. So why now? Why this year? Why tonight when the new rules were supposedly in effect?

"Relax, dude," Toby said, leaning back against the passenger seat of the Sentra, "they'll be here."

"They're bringing the beer? You're sure?"

"Yeah, yeah, I'm sure."

"They better not bring Colt 45 or Schlitz or something."

"Why, what do you drink, Cristal?"

"No, it's just . . . never mind."

"The point is to get hammered before we go in there. My advice is to have a few drinks at home first. That's what I do. Otherwise who could face it? I'm asking you. The music, the lame decorations and the weak punch and cookies. It's a joke. The jocks, the nerds, the goths all hanging in their own little ghettos. It can be brutal. But I don't have to tell you that. You've been to these things before, right?" Toby asked.

Maybe Toby had been so involved with his former girl-friend, the one with the tattoos and the piercings, he hadn't noticed if Rich was there or not. It was time Toby found some new guy friends. Rich was just too dorky, Jared was too pushy and Steve was too full of himself.

"Not really," Rich said. "Not a mixer. But I thought . . . I mean we're juniors, high school's half over and how many more of these deals are left for us? My brother said I have to get out more. Meet people. You know any girls who'll be there?"

Toby shot a glance at Richard. So that's what this was about. Richard's family had made him come tonight. They'd always leaned on him to be more social. They'd pushed him to be friends with Toby since they were in grade school. Or maybe Rich had a crush on some girl and was hoping to hook up with her tonight. Or maybe it was both. Toby felt a pain in his chest that was probably just heartburn from the can of chili he'd eaten at home by himself. Or maybe it was a rush of nostalgia. It couldn't be envy, could it?

He used to have parents who cared what he did. He used to like girls. A long time ago when he was young—sixteen. No more. Maybe he'd be back in the game next year, but not now. Then why was he here? What was the choice? Where was he supposed to be on a Saturday night? At home alone?

"Will they know if we've been drinking? Is it true they're gonna be checking at the door?" Richard asked, gripping the steering wheel with white knuckles. "Don't forget about the new headmaster. He sounds strict."

"Strict? He sounds like a dictator, not a headmaster," Toby said, knowing full well it was parents like Richard's who'd helped get the last laissez-faire headmaster fired. "But Jesus, Richard, you don't have to drink if you don't want to. If you're that worried . . ."

"I know. I want to, I just . . ."

Just then Steve Heller and Jared pulled up in Steve's rebuilt Mustang, looking as cool as if they'd just stepped out of *That '70s Show*. Maybe Toby's dad would cough up a muscle car like that for his birthday now that money wasn't so tight. It would be easy to pick up girls in a car like that. Not that Toby wanted to pick up girls until he recovered from that last disaster, but if he did someday . . .

Steve, the school's basketball star, got out of the Mustang and waved a six-pack of Miller Lite in the air.

"You got Miller Lite?" Richard got out of the car, clearly disgusted with the choice of beverage.

That's right, diss Steve's taste in beer, Toby thought. Good way to make friends, which Rich could stand to do. Toby joined the newcomers outside between the two cars. Maybe Steve was trying to make a statement with the Miller Lite. Maybe he was sick of those fancy dark imports. Who cared as long as it was alcohol?

Jared stood up and threw up his hands in mock disgust. "He wanted to get forties of Olde English. I had to twist his arm to get this."

Steve, who brimmed with confidence on and off the court, laughed. "Sometimes I just like to go slumming. We started with the good stuff an hour ago."

"Where should we go to drink it?" Richard asked, twisting his head around at a pair of headlights just entering the parking lot.

"Behind Archer Hall," Steve and Jared said in unison. The Hall was named for the Archer family, who'd erected the building in gratitude after several of their IQ-challenged progeny finally squeaked through and graduated from Manderley.

Archer Hall was the best place to hide out, day or night, with the smallest chance of sabotage by teachers or security guards. At least it was last year. Toby had a funny feeling tonight. Like things weren't the same. It wasn't just the new headmaster. It was something else. A weird knot in his stomach he couldn't shake. His head was pounding and he felt queasy. Maybe he shouldn't drink any more tonight. But then how could he possibly have a good time?

Archer Hall had become famous after it was voted the best place to have sex on campus in a poll taken for the underground student newspaper last year. Second place went to the girls' locker room at the swimming pool. On those hard narrow benches? Toby tried to picture it, but couldn't. There had to be a better place.

The guys settled on the dark patch of grass behind the Greek classic–style hall. There in the dark they cracked open the six-pack and pounded it, as if in training for future pledging of frats at college.

"Lemme go check out the scene," Jared said after chugging two cans in a row. "See who's there before we waste any money buying tickets. Check out the hotties, you know what I mean? If there aren't any, this could be an event we want to miss. Especially if the general has ordered a dress code. That could be a disaster."

He and Richard stumbled off around the building toward the gym. Toby stifled the urge to tell them to watch out for the headmaster and his goons who might be at the door. They ought to know that. If they got caught, they'd all have to split.

After drinking his second Miller Lite in two loud, gigantic swallows, Steve tossed his empty can and he and Toby walked slowly toward the gym where they bumped into Jared.

"We're screwed," he said. "They've got a Breathalyzer and they're checking everyone at the door. Anyone got any ideas?"

"Who's doing the checking?" Steve asked.

"The new headmaster, what's his name, General Kavanaugh. And a tall redheaded girl who's at the door too. Cindy something."

Toby stumbled on the damp grass. "Not Cindy something," he mumbled. "Cindy Ellis." He should have known. She was everywhere he went. First she was assigned to be his partner. Then she decided what their paper was going to be on. After that she made him go see his grandfather who hardly knew who he was. Now she'd joined the administration and had some role in deciding who could get in and who couldn't? He couldn't believe it. What next? Where did it end? If he had any sense he'd go home now. "I'm outta here," he said.

"You can't go now," Steve said. "Not if you've got a connection with this Cindy."

"No, he can't," Jared said. "Not until he gets us in the gym."

"I can't get us in. I don't even want to get in," Toby protested. "I'm sick. I'm going home."

"Tell your girlfriend to let us in first, then go home," Jared said.

"I don't have a girlfriend, and if I did, it wouldn't be her," Toby said, popping a breath mint in his mouth.

"Okay, she's not your girlfriend, but you know her. She's in your history class, isn't she?" Jared said. He shoved his face into Toby's and exhaled so much alcoholic breath that Toby felt his blood-alcohol level jump. "All you have to do is distract her while we get by the Breathalyzer."

"And how am I supposed to do that?"

"Ask her something. Ask her to the homecoming dance."

"Are you out of your freaking mind?" Toby demanded.

"Okay, ask her something else, like what's your history homework. It doesn't matter. Then introduce me. I want to meet her," Jared insisted.

"Let me get this straight," Toby said, dumbfounded. He must be losing his hearing from keeping his iPod turned up so loud. "You want to meet Cindy Ellis. You're interested in her, the tall, red-haired geeky girl? Why?"

"Because of her sisters. The Vanderhoffer twins."

"The blond cheerleaders?" Toby blinked. "Those are Cindy Ellis's sisters?"

"Stepsisters. How come you don't know that? I thought we could double date."

"Oh, right, brilliant idea, Jared. You and I and those twins. First, they're seniors. Second, they're sluts. But they're choosy sluts. They only do athletes like Steve here."

"Leave me outta this," Steve said. "I'm saving myself for a virgin."

"Not you and me and the twins, dude," Jared said, ignoring Steve's obvious joke. He slapped Toby on the arm. "You go out with Cindy and I take one of the twins. Either one. Rich here can have the other. I hear they do this thing with their knees . . ."

Rich muttered something unintelligible and Toby laughed

so hard at the preposterous mental image of himself with Cindy and Jared and Rich each with one of the twins, he fell down and rolled around on the grass.

"Oh, man," he said, holding his sides so his stomach wouldn't revolt. "You're killing me."

nineteen

On with the dance! let joy be unconfin'd;
No sleep till morn, when Youth and Pleasure meet
To chase the glowing hours with flying feet.

—<u>Childe Harold's Pilgrimage</u>, Lord Byron

Cindy liked selling tickets. It gave her something to do. She felt useful. She got to see who was with who even though she didn't know many of the names. Best of all she didn't feel like an outsider. She even saw a few kids she knew, like Victoria, who gave her a ride to the dance with another Chinese girl, and Scott, her friend from geometry. Maybe going inside the gym after selling tickets wouldn't be so bad. Even though she'd be bombasted by the DJ's choice of ear-splitting music while pouring punch for ungrateful students.

Just when she was congratulating herself on being part of a social function without the stress of having to look like she was having a good time, the new headmaster, who was checking students at the next door for any alcohol consumption, spotted a couple freak-dancing on the other side of the gym.

He came up to Cindy, eyes bulging, his throat constricted so that Cindy was afraid he was going to explode. Perhaps such behavior hadn't occurred at Cuthbert. But Cuthbert was hardly some kind of Amish school where the girls wore long dresses and bonnets and the boys drove a team of horses instead of sports cars. What kind of dancing did they do at Cuthbert? The Macarena?

Cindy admitted if the man had never seen freak dancing, and if the couple weren't wearing clothes, (if you can call a micro-miniskirt and a bare midriff clothes), he might have thought they were having sex right on the dance floor. Maybe that's what he did think. After all, it was pretty dark in there.

"Here," he said to Cindy when he found his voice. "Take my Breathalyzer and check everyone out. I'll be right back as soon as I put a stop to this. It's the music. It makes students behave like animals. This is just disgusting."

"But wait," Cindy said, holding the Breathalyzer out away from her body like a lethal weapon. "I don't know how to use this."

"The student blows through the mouthpiece for five seconds. The sensors here measure the alcohol level of air in the lungs. It's simple enough to do."

"But what numbers . . ."

"There's no acceptable level. Any number that shows up is too much. Don't let them in." With that he stomped off across the room while Cindy stood in the doorway watching him push his way between couples rocking to Gwen Stefani's song "Hollaback Girl."

This was ridiculous. There was no way she could sell tickets *and* make anyone take a Breathalyzer test. Even if she did and they failed, how would she make them leave? They'd just laugh at her and go in anyway.

Speaking of laughing, Cindy was not amused to have her sisters arrive at that moment with their cheerleader clique. They were talking about the soccer match that afternoon against their rival, Saint Paul. If Cindy hadn't had to work at the salon she might have . . . what, gone to the game? It was in another town. She might as well wish to go to the World Cup in Germany. While waiting in the ticket line, they talked non-stop about Marco. The goals he made, the goals he saved, the kicks he made, the assists, the red cards, the penalties. Cindy was well aware of the team members' not-so-friendly rivalry with each other, which extended both to their cheerleading stunts as well as to who had the inside track with Marco.

"What are you doing here?" Brie asked Cindy when she stopped talking long enough to realize who was selling tickets.

Cindy wanted to say, *I go to school here, remember? I go to dances and games and join clubs . . . or I could if I had time to.* Of course she didn't. Instead she said, "Selling tickets and . . ." Tell her sisters about the Breathalyzer test? No way. "You know, just hanging out," she added weakly.

"Well, don't hang out around us," Brie said, giving Cindy a brisk once-over to make sure she wasn't wearing any of her clothes.

Hang out around that crowd? Cindy would rather hang out with a group of serial killers.

"Who's that?" one of their friends asked Lauren, pointing a long red fingernail at Cindy.

Lauren shrugged. "Her? Nobody. Trust me, she's nobody you'd want to know."

"Let's go," Brie said impatiently, slapping a wad of dollar bills into Cindy's hand and leaning into the doorway of the gym "I love this DJ. He looks just like the rapper Nelly with the same tattoos and the Band-Aid on one cheek. I'm going to request that Paris Hilton song, 'Stars Are Blind.' She actually has an album, you know."

Cindy was glad to see them disappear into the dark cavern of the gym where the theme was Water World. Blue water-based wallpaper from some party store was stapled onto the walls. Cardboard fish cutouts hung from the ceilings. If only one of those cardboard sharks could come to life and swallow up her sisters. That would be worth the price of admission.

The DJ was now playing a song by the Killers way too loudly. Or maybe it was the Strokes. Brie and Lauren would know. They'd been playing those songs nonstop at home until Cindy had to use her earplugs to do her homework.

She paused long enough to see Mr. Jefferson, the fat science teacher, stuffing himself with cookies from the snack table while eyeing the dancers suspiciously. But she didn't see the headmaster anywhere. Maybe the dancers had been tipped off and had retreated before he caught them. According to her sisters, Jefferson made a habit of humiliating students who weren't paying attention in class. Cindy would like to see anyone try to humiliate those two. They could give lessons in humiliation techniques.

She cringed at how tacky the whole scene was. Somehow she'd imagined the fall Welcome Dance at Manderley would have talented live musicians and tasteful decorations in autumn colors. Maybe she'd give up and go home after her stint at the door.

The next group to arrive was her brain-dead partner Toby, who she now knew was a well-known slacker, with his friends and the blond athlete Steve, who Victoria would be excited to see. She could smell the alcohol on all of them. No Breathalyzer test needed, but what was she supposed to do? How could she make them leave?

"Um, have you guys been drinking?" she asked.

"Who, us?" said one of Toby's friends while Toby stood there looking pretty much like he always did, totally out of it. "Of course not."

Cindy peeked into the gym again, but the headmaster was still MIA. In fact the dancing had deteriorated even further. The DJ was now playing a rap song, and the students were bumping and grinding and freaking on each other. Toby and the guys he was with bought their tickets and walked into the dance as if they were sober while Cindy watched helplessly for a few minutes, then turned around and sold more tickets.

Suddenly the music changed. The lights on the dance floor blazed. Students froze in place. The DJ who'd deserted his post and had been dancing with one of the twins stopped abruptly and stood openmouthed in disbelief. No wonder. The song that filled the gym was the theme song from Barney.

> *Barney comes to play with us.*
> *Whenever we may need him.*

The new headmaster was no longer checking for alcohol consumption. He'd taken over as the DJ. Who else would have the nerve to do it?

twenty

*If A is success in life, then A equals X plus Y. Work is
X, Y is play, and Z is keeping your mouth shut.*

—Albert Einstein

After that, everything was a blur. Even for Cindy, who hadn't had
a drop to drink except for a sip of the fruit punch. After a brief
pause, the lights went down again, the DJ was back, playing mopey
but danceable rock music while the headmaster went on another
mission. After his success in changing the music, he turned to the
one thing he'd most wanted to do before he got sidetracked.

This time he was concentrating on rooting out all the students who'd somehow gotten in with alcohol on their breath.
Cindy didn't know how he found them in the crush, but the
first to get the boot were Toby's friends. Toby's friends, but no
Toby. How had he escaped the headmaster's wrath?

The headmaster pulled the guys outside and began dialing on his cell phone.

"I'm calling your parents to come and get you," he said, lining them up and taking their names and numbers just like he no doubt had done in the Marine Corps.

"Wait, I'm safe to drive," one of them said. "I just blew a point-zero-eight on the Breathalyzer."

"Oh, no you're not," Kavanaugh said. "There is no acceptable level of consumption that makes it safe to drive. I'm not having a potential accident happen on my watch. Any alcohol that enters a person's body can impair reflexes, motor skills and cognitive abilities." The man sounded like he was reading from a manual.

Cindy could have told him those guys probably didn't have much in the way of cognitive abilities anyway, except for Steve, but she kept her opinions to herself as she'd been taught.

"Need some help?"

Cindy whirled around. She knew that voice, that accent. Yes, it was Marco, looking more gorgeous than ever. Under the mercury light above the school entrance she could see he wore perfectly fitted clothes straight out of *GQ*, the Italian version. Which made her even more conscious of her own old but carefully ironed jeans and her blue silk shirt, another hand-me-down. Now she wished she'd borrowed some better clothes and let Scott cut her hair as he'd offered. Too late.

"Hello, Marco," Kavanaugh said with a smile. It may have

been the first time he'd smiled since he came to Manderley. "Nice to see you. You played a magnificent game today."

"Thank you, sir," Marco said.

"First time Manderley has beaten Saint Paul for three years. Just shows what we can do with some decent talent and a little extra money thrown at athletics."

Marco shot a glance at the group of miscreants. "Can I be of some help?" he asked.

"I'm sending some students home. Students who willfully ignored my warning about drinking. Naturally they can't drive."

"I would be happy to drive them home. The van the team took to the game is parked in the lot out there and I still have the keys if you think . . ."

"That's very generous of you. Thank you, Marco, but I'm afraid you'll miss part of the dance."

"*Non importa*," he said with a smile. "It doesn't matter. The dance will still be here when I return, no?"

"Of course."

"I see my tutor is here," he said with a devastating smile.

Cindy smiled weakly. "Hi, Marco," she said.

"Can you come along with me? Ride along as my, how do you say . . ."

"Co-pilot?" she suggested as her heart thumped so loudly she was sure everyone could hear it above the loud music.

"*Si, andiamo*," Marco said.

Cindy looked at the headmaster. He looked at her. There was a long pause. She held her breath. Did she need his permission? But the moment passed before she could act. Too late. Too late.

Her sisters, whose antennae had somehow detected the hottest guy around was outside, rushed out of the gym and almost ran her over in their excitement. They enveloped Marco in hugs and congratulations for a game well played. While Cindy watched, Brie, Lauren, Marco, a few other random kids and Toby's friends disappeared into the night, trailing laughter behind them.

Marco turned to look back at her. It was too dark to see his face clearly. What was he thinking? That she didn't want to go? That she was too shy, too hesitant, not enough of a rebel to push her way in, to insist on sitting next to him as his co-pilot? If he thought that, he was right.

Cindy stood there, deserted and alone while everyone else went off to have fun. It was her own fault. She could have gone. The music came wafting out of the gym. The song they were playing? Daniel Powter's "Bad Day."

twenty-one

There are two things in life for which we are truly never prepared: twins.

—Josh Billings

Toby crawled across the wet grass in the dark and watched his friends get into the new sports van while the music faded into the background. For once he'd escaped, thanks to his weak stomach. If he'd been on the dance floor when the Nazi had busted his friends, then he'd be with them now, on his way home with the Vanderhoffer twins. Wait a minute. How did that happen? Had they been drinking too? Who hadn't? Should he have crawled after them and confessed so he wouldn't be left out?

Jared must be in hog heaven. Squeezed into the van with the girls of his dreams. In between the two of them, if dreams really did come true. If the rumors were valid, God only knew what Jared would get out of the ride to his house, besides a ride to his house.

Even in the dark he could see the twins were wearing dresses that used to be worn only by prostitutes, but which must have cost in the three-digits. And yet Cindy, their so-called stepsister, was wearing some denims and a shirt that was a size too big for her. What a contrast.

He'd never be able to explain to his friends why he'd escaped getting caught. He didn't want anyone to know that he'd gone outside to throw up in the bushes. What a way to end a perfect day.

Was it any better to be lying on the grass, feeling physically wretched but spared from having some Italian jock pull up in front of his house and have the neighbors see him stumble out like he'd just been let out of prison?

Yes!

In a few minutes, or a few hours, he'd work his way to the parking lot and find a way home. He didn't know why he'd even come tonight. The whole thing had been totally lame, starting with Rich and ending with him alone and flat on his face. He wondered drunkenly if he should give up alcohol. He couldn't seem to drink anymore without getting sick. Classes went by in a haze. Friends came and went. Or were they really friends? What was the point of making an effort for them like he had tonight?

Maybe he should give up high school too. That might be harder to do unless he could get his father or mother to home-school him. Fat chance.

There were no girls at this school that excited him. Take the Vanderhoffer twins at one end of the hot scale and their stepsister, Cindy, queen of the geeks, at the other end. The dances had never been much fun, but they'd gone from tame and over-chaperoned to stupid events out of a Manga book like the dance tonight.

When his cell phone rang and he saw it was Jared, it was only a dull curiosity that made him answer.

"Where are you, man?" Jared said.

"You know, still here, hanging with my homies," Toby lied, getting to his knees. "What happened to you?" As if he didn't know.

"You don't know? We decided to cut out early. Couldn't find you. You'll never guess who gave us a ride home."

"Are they tall and blond and have a sister?" Toby asked.

"Shit. How did you know?"

"Just a lucky guess. How did that happen?"

"I don't know. I guess I've just got what it takes. Girls can't get enough of me. Once those hotties saw me they were all over me like I was the new Double-Oh-Seven or something."

"You were lucky to fight them off, I guess." Toby finally got to his feet and walked slowly and unsteadily toward the parking lot. The more Jared bragged, the better Toby felt about his escape. And the happier he was he hadn't taken a ride with them. And the more he thought about stopping drinking. Oh, not altogether, just cutting back a little. At least for now. To see if it made any difference.

"Yeah, okay, talk to you later. Gotta go now."

Toby could hear Jared's dad yelling in the background and Toby wasn't sure if he missed having a dad around who cared if he got drunk or if he was happy to be on his own. If he did stop drinking, it wouldn't be to please his father; his father didn't know or care. He had to do it for himself. There wasn't anyone else.

Only thing was, how was he going to get home?

twenty-two

Demons don't play by the rules.
They lie and they cheat and they stab in the back.

—Alan Grant

By the time the twins got home from the dance, Cindy was in bed, but no earplugs existed that could keep out their loud laughter and shrieks of glee at the fun they'd had. Cindy buried her head under the blankets but could not block out the sounds reverberating throughout the house. The whole neighborhood must have heard how they'd danced, drank, partied and played.

She wondered if Marco had spent the rest of the evening freak-dancing with them when they returned to the dance, or if the headmaster had put a stop to their fun with the Barney songs and they'd moved on to another venue like some friend's McMansion with no parents at home. She told herself it was just as well she hadn't gone with them. But sometimes she wondered what would have happened if she had.

The next day Marco called her on her cell phone while she was working at the spa. She was so shocked she almost dropped the pumice stone she used to scrub the clients' feet with.

"How did you get my number?" she asked, taking refuge in the supply closet so Irina wouldn't know she was taking a personal call, a total no-no for spa employees.

"It was on the tutor list with your name. I'm sorry to bother you. You're busy, yes?"

"Well, yes, I'm at work."

"What about lunch? Can you meet me for lunch?"

"I . . . I don't know." Irina gave her fifteen minutes to eat a sandwich unless the place was really busy, then she worked straight through until the spa closed. "Is it something that can't wait until school on Monday?"

He didn't answer. Instead he asked her, "What kind of a job doesn't let you have time for lunch? In Italy it would be a crime. Everything closes at noon. We eat, we talk, we rest. Then we go back to work."

"But we're not in Italy," she said. "Unfortunately."

"I will come there. I will bring the lunch. It's the least I can do for you who helps me so much."

"Here? No. Okay, I'll meet you in the mall at the tables in front of the Oakton Grocery. Do you know where that is?"

"I will find it. I will be there at twelve."

Cindy nodded and hung up just as Irina was banging on the closet door, demanding to know what Cindy was doing in there. Cindy left feeling guilty about leaving the customer whose feet were still soaking in a cocoa bath, her skin turning brown and wrinkled as she dozed in her massage chair. Never mind; her skin would ultimately be soft as a baby's.

Marco was pacing back and forth in front of the upscale grocery where he'd just purchased two proscuitto and Fontina cheese sandwiches and two bottles of San Pellegrino water. He hoped Cindy wouldn't be in trouble for taking time from her job, but really what kind of a country was this that didn't give workers time to eat a proper meal at noon?

When he saw her she was walking quickly toward him, her copper-colored hair shining in the autumn sunlight. She was different from any other girl he'd ever met. She was hardworking, both at school and at her job. She was shy and she didn't seem to have any idea how attractive she was, with her beautiful cheekbones like Sophia Loren's and a wide mouth that curved up when she was amused. He liked to make her smile. He'd like to make her laugh too. Of course her clothes were terrible. She didn't seem to know or care. That was refreshing.

He restrained himself from kissing her on both cheeks as he

would have when meeting a friend in Italy. He just motioned for her to sit down and opened the plastic tray with the sandwiches.

She took a bite of her sandwich. "This is delicious," she said.

"I'm glad you like it. I had to come and apologize," he said.

Her eyes widened.

"For last night. I invited you to come along in the car, then I left you behind."

She shook her head. "You didn't leave me, I left myself."

"No, it was my fault. When I returned to the dance, you were gone. I didn't have a chance to dance with you."

"It's just as well. I'm not much of a dancer."

"But I am. I could have taught you."

"How was it? I hope the headmaster didn't have to stop the dance again."

"I'm not sure. I left too. It seemed like there was no reason to stay any longer." He'd been anxious to make things right with Cindy. When she was gone, he had looked around and hadn't seen anyone he wanted to talk to or dance with. The room had been full of loud and immature teenagers, but it might as well have been empty.

He reached for her hand across the table. "Thank you for meeting me here today."

"Thank you for the lunch." She looked around. "Is this what it's like eating slowly outside in Italy?"

"Yes," he said, leaning back in his chair and smiling at her. "But at my house, we'd be having three courses. Next time I'll try to manage that." He didn't know until he said it that there would be a next time. He didn't realize how pleasant it was to share a lunch with his tutor. He knew she was different from other girls, *piacevole*, patient and smart. He didn't know how much he liked her until that moment.

He walked her back to the salon where she worked, then he went to Manderley for soccer practice. While he was changing into his soccer shoes he wondered what it would be like to have an American girlfriend. It probably wasn't a good idea even though it wouldn't be bad for his English. It would only be short-term. He had no idea where he'd be next year. Probably back in Italy, unless his grades, his soccer skill and his English were good enough to get him into an American university. A girlfriend, even one as intriguing as Cindy, would just be a distraction now. But he was tempted. And Marco wasn't used to resisting temptation.

twenty-three

A kiss that's never tasted, is forever and ever wasted.

—Billie Holiday

On Monday morning Cindy was in the twins' car and she was once again a captive audience, listening to them rant about their college application essays.

"Cindy, you're a good writer. You can write them for us."

"That would be cheating," Cindy said primly from her usual seat behind them in the jeep.

"Flash!" Lauren said to Brie. "That's cheating. Did you hear that, Brie?"

"Look, smart-ass, you owe us something," Lauren said.

"For what?" Cindy asked. *For letting her sleep in a closet under the stairs? For not kicking her out of the house and sending her to a foster home? For working at the spa all summer while they were at Cheer Camp?*

"For everything we've done for you. Driving you to school, for one thing. Giving you the clothes off our backs, for another. For letting you go to our school. You're probably wondering why anyone's nice to you at all, being such a geek. Here's why. Because they think you'll put in a good word for them with us. As if."

"I'm not writing the essays for you," Cindy said with a new-found determination. "But I'll look at them and make suggestions if you want."

"Look at them?" Brie asked. "There's nothing to look at. Just blank pages. How're we supposed to know what to write?"

"Write about what's important to you." *Boys, booze, clothes, yourselves.* "What makes you special, different from everyone else."

"Like cheerleading," Lauren said.

"That's good," Cindy said. "Write about how dangerous it is, how challenging. Explain why you do it instead of something else." *Something worthwhile like helping refugees in Darfur or taking care of sick children in Romania.*

"But we both can't write the same essay," Lauren said, her pouty lips turned down.

"That's a problem," Cindy said trying to hide a smile.

"Please?" Brie said. "You're so good at it. Just write two little essays about cheerleading for us?"

Cindy sighed. When was the last time either one of them had said the word *please*? She was too tired to argue anymore. And what good would it do?

"Okay," she said. But she was mad at herself for giving in. This was it. The last time she'd let them push her around.

At least she gave them each an assignment to write a rough draft of their essay. They grumbled, and she realized even that was asking too much of them and they probably wouldn't bother.

The person she really wanted to help had sent her a note canceling his session with her. Since their lunch Saturday she had been looking forward to seeing him with breathless anticipation.

Ciao, bella, he'd written in a note he handed her on Monday. Being called beautiful in Italian gave her a funny little feeling in the pit of her stomach.

Scusi, *he went on,* but I am how to say purtroppo? not able to see you for the tutoring next Friday because of the soccer game which requires me. Coach tells me he likes the way I play. "Ruthless, aggressive and without mercy," *he says. I looked up these words in my Italian dictionary and I guess he's right. That's how we win in soccer or poker too. Do you agree? You know if I am a rebel, but am I really like this?* Tu amico fedele, *Marco.*

Never having seen Marco play soccer or poker, Cindy had no idea if he was ruthless or without mercy when playing. Trying to hide her disappointment, she then changed her schedule to work in the dean's office Friday after school, though her friends at Castle wanted her to do something with them. Her stepmother also demanded that she work for her, but Cindy put her off. And there was that soccer game. Victoria wanted Cindy to go with her. But Marco hadn't even suggested that she go to it. Was that because he didn't think the game was important or thought that she wasn't important?

Yes, he'd bought her lunch, but that wasn't a date. It was just because he felt guilty for leaving her out after the dance. She told herself a sandwich was just a sandwich, as much as she wished it was more than that.

twenty-four

Always tell the truth. That way, you don't have to remember what you said.

—Mark Twain

On Friday afternoon Cindy was putting in her work-study hours. The school offices were empty since the staff members had either gone home or were at the soccer game. There was a warm breeze wafting through the quiet office on the first floor of the mansion. Cindy tried to imagine what life was like when Gertrude Manderley had lived there, entertaining her feminist bluestocking friends, smoking cigars and discussing the latest literary or political figures. Her cell phone rang.

"Cindy," Lizzie said. "We're going to the beach today. I'll come by your rich snob school to pick you up."

"I can't. I have to work in the office."

"Work? Nobody works after school on a Friday."

"I know, but I owe them certain hours and since my tutoring session got canceled . . ."

"Is it that cute Toby you're tutoring?"

"He's not that cute and I'm not tutoring him. No, it's someone else." It wasn't that long ago that Cindy used to tell her BFF everything. Now she was keeping Marco a secret. Why? Because she was afraid they'd tell her she was a hopeless dreamer? She already knew that. "And then there's a soccer game I might go to. It's the first home game of the season."

"Soccer? You've never been interested in organized sports before."

If she wanted to keep Marco a secret, Toby might make a good decoy. It was about time he was good for something.

"Well, Toby might be there." It wasn't a lie. He probably would be there. As long as he was somewhere across the field, she could point to him. *That's Toby*, she'd say. And Lizzie would understand. As long as he didn't come up close and she could see what he was really like.

"I get it," Lizzie said. "Come with us for once. You never have time for us anymore. New school, new friends, new boyfriend. What about us?"

"I'm sorry, but . . . I wish I could go but I can't," Cindy said. Why go on about the increased workload at this school, the new point system, her stepmother's spa and work-study. It wouldn't do any good. Lizzie just didn't understand.

"You can if you want to. I'm going home to get Buzz. He loves to run on the beach."

"See, you've got a dog. And friends. You don't need me."

"Yeah, but you need us. See you in a while."

"No, wait, Liz, I can't go with you." But she'd hung up. Cindy gave a frustrated sigh. Her friends just didn't understand how quickly her free time was sucked up.

First, none of them was an orphan. Second, not one of them was here at Manderley where there were high expectations and a heavy homework load and new rules every day. And third, they didn't tutor or have a demanding stepmother who owned a spa. Also, she didn't want her old friends to come to the soccer game. They might guess she had a hopeless crush on Marco. Which was why she was going to use Toby if she had to.

Also, Lizzie and the BFF would instantly see how different life was on the other side of town and they'd wonder out loud how she could stand it. They'd either be envious or they'd feel sorry for her.

How was she going to reconcile her two worlds? Wasn't it better not to even try? She was at Manderley now and there was no going back to her old life.

She tried to call Lizzie back but she didn't answer. Cindy left her a message.

"Liz, I really can't go anywhere today. After I work here I have to go to the spa and fold towels or Irina will hit the roof.

Thanks for asking me. You know how I love the beach, but maybe some other day?"

Cindy didn't know what day that would be. She felt terrible lying to her best friend, but wasn't lying better than hurting someone's feelings?

twenty-five

My grandmother started walking five miles a day when she was sixty. She's ninety-seven now, and we don't know where the hell she is.

—Ellen DeGeneres

Cindy went back to her filing until she heard the sharp sound of a woman's voice in the hall speaking a foreign language. After having listened in secret to several Italian language tapes, Cindy knew enough to almost understand a few words. Especially when those words were "Marco Valenti."

The next thing she knew a tiny old woman dressed in a long black dress and black shoes with her hair pulled back from her small, wrinkled face entered the office and pounded her cane on the polished floorboards. "Marco Valenti," she said loudly. *"Desidero vedere il mio nipote!"*

Cindy dropped a folder and the papers inside it scattered.

131

She was so stunned she just stood and stared at her. The woman stared back and repeated the sentence more loudly this time. Her dark eyes glittered. Then she waved her cane in the air. She was obviously frustrated, but who was she and what did she want? She wanted Marco, of course.

There was only one person who knew for sure. One person who could understand her. And he was playing in a crucial soccer match today. At least that's what the student newspaper said.

Cindy smiled encouragingly and pointed to a chair. The old woman shook her head. Cindy reached for her pocket Italian dictionary in her backpack and quickly thumbed through it.

Then she spoke clearly and slowly with what must have been a horrible accent, *"Ciao. State cercando il vostro nipote?"* Hello. Are you looking for your grandson?

"Si," the woman said, then burst into a long tirade as if Cindy could understand her.

Cindy nodded. Then she grabbed her backpack and her clarinet, took the old lady's arm and led her down the steps and across the grass toward the field. All the while Marco's grandmother never stopped talking. Now where had she come from out of the blue? Sometimes she appeared to ask Cindy a question, which Cindy didn't understand, of course. Cindy could only continue to smile until her face hurt. She hoped the grandmother didn't think she was being rude by not talking. Had that one sentence convinced her that Cindy actually spoke and understood Italian?

The soccer field was on the other side of campus but the cheers and shouts from the students carried across the green lawns. Cindy felt her heart rate speed up. Soccer must be exciting after all. Or was it Marco who made it exciting? She had a feeling he could make checkers exciting.

She was surprised at how fast the old lady walked, with her cane in one hand, a handbag over one arm and her other hand on Cindy's arm. As if she knew where they were going and why. It was as if she didn't want to miss a minute of her grandson's performance. Cindy understood that.

The field was clear of players, but Cindy saw her sisters performing their gymnastics in front of the stands with their team. As they jumped and twisted to the music, high-kicking and showing off their curvy streamlined bodies, she had to admit it took some talent and a lot of energy. But Marco's grandmother's eyes widened. She pointed at them and shook her head, her forehead creased in a frown.

"Prostitute! Difettosi delle ragazzi," she said. Good thing she didn't know those girls were semi-related to her.

Cindy found a space in the front row of the bleachers for Marco's grandmother and herself and they sat down quickly without her scanning the stands to see if she recognized anyone she knew. If his grandmother attracted curious glances for even a moment, Cindy didn't want to know about it. Anyway, when the game resumed, everyone's attention went back to the players who were racing up and down the field.

Even Cindy, who'd never seen a soccer game before, caught the fever. She saw instantly that Marco was the star. He kicked the ball down the field, making his way steadily through a crowd of players who were trying with no success to stop him and take his ball away. He looked as if he'd hardly broken a sweat. Aggressive? Definitely. Ruthless? Not that she could tell.

The home crowd roared their approval as he kicked a goal. They copied the Europeans and shouted "goooooal." There was scarcely a break before the action began once again. And once again it was Marco who got the ball and began another trip to the goal posts. He made it look so effortless. Maybe it was.

His grandmother saw him before he saw her. The old lady dropped her cane, stood without help and shouted, *"Marco, mi caro nipote piccolo!"*

How Marco ever heard his grandmother's voice with all the shouting going on, Cindy never knew. It was clear, however, that he did hear her. He'd just bounced the ball off his head to a team member when he glanced over at the stand where they were sitting, saw them, and looked as startled as if he'd been struck by lightning. Cindy wasn't sure if it was just surprise or dismay. Whatever it was, he lost his concentration and his sense of direction. Not only that, he almost lost the ball to the other team who, sensing his distraction, rushed him.

Marco's grandmother got to her feet and started walking

toward the field. Cindy jumped to her feet and went after her. For a woman her age, she had surprising speed. Maybe that's where Marco got it.

Cindy wondered if she'd ever seen a game before. Didn't she know she couldn't get any closer? Apparently not, because the old woman was one step from walking right onto the field when Cindy caught her and put one restraining hand on her frail shoulder.

Cindy never saw the ball come at her. She did hear the roar of the crowd. And she felt the vibrations in the air. The next thing she knew she'd been hit on the side of the head with a loud *smack* that sent her sprawling onto the soft ground, and everything went black.

twenty-six

There are no accidents. God's just trying to remain anony-mous.

—Brett Butler

When Cindy came to, she was lying on her back under a tree. Her head was pounding and when she opened her eyes in little slits, everything was bright and blurry. She thought she saw a whole group of slightly familiar faces. If they hadn't looked so concerned and spoken in such hushed voices, she would have thought she'd died and gone to heaven. If so, they spoke Italian in heaven. Why not?

"Cio é tutto il mio difetto. Nonna, che cosa state facendo qui?"

"Marco, sono venuto vederti. Non avete risposto mai alla mia lettera."

"Is she going to be okay?" someone asked in English.

"Who is she?"

"Did anyone call nine-one-one?"

Cindy's eyes flew open. 9ll? They couldn't do that. An ambulance would come. She'd be taken off on a stretcher. Sirens would sound. It would be so embarrassing. This was bad enough. Cindy forced herself to sit up.

"I'm fine," she said weakly. "I just got bumped on the head."

"It was my fault," Marco said.

So it really was him, his sweaty face looking solemn and concerned as he leaned forward and looked deep into her eyes. She felt a tremor hit her whole body. Good thing she was already on the ground, or she would have fallen.

"She's in shock. Somebody get a jacket."

Before anyone could offer a jacket, Marco's grandmother had produced a warm black shawl from her handbag and wrapped it around Cindy's shoulders.

"Really, I'm okay," Cindy said.

"She's okay," Marco said. "Everybody go back to the game. Give her some air. I'm taking her home."

Voices rose in protest.

"But, Marco, we need you."

"Marco, we'll lose without you."

He looked at his watch. "Only two minutes left. You can play without me." His voice was firm. The star had spoken.

While Cindy was waiting for Marco to bring his car to the

field, she knew she really wasn't okay. She was delirious. Also she must be hallucinating. The aggressive, play-without-mercy Marco Valenti was taking her home before the game was over? She could hear the cheers echoing in the crisp fall air. Was the two minutes up? Had they won? She hoped so.

She could imagine her sisters leaping in the air, their hair standing on end, or doing cartwheels, walkovers and back tucks while they celebrated another victory. Maybe she'd short-changed them. Maybe they had more skill than she'd given them credit for. She sat there, wrapped in a black shawl, her back against an old tree with Marco's grandmother standing next to her, waving people away like some ancient chaperone from another era and muttering in Italian.

"Cindy." Cindy turned her head slowly to see Lizzie with her dog on a leash. "I'm glad I found you. I thought you had to work. What's wrong?"

"Nothing. I got hit with a ball, that's all."

"Are you ready? Let's go."

"Uh, no. I don't think so. I feel a little funny."

Lizzie sat down next to Cindy and hugged her knees to her chest. "You look funny. What are you gonna do? Do you want me to take you home?"

"Somebody already volunteered. You go on to the beach. I'll be fine."

Lizzie glanced up at the strange little figure standing there dressed in black. "Who's that?" she whispered.

"She's someone's grandmother," Cindy said.

"Yeah, I guessed that. But whose? And what's she doing here?"

"I . . . uh . . . I'll explain later. And you don't have to whisper. She doesn't speak English."

"I thought you had to work."

"I did." Cindy sighed. "It's a long story and my head hurts."

Just then Marco pulled up in his Alfa Romeo and Cindy got Liz to help her stand.

"Who's that?" Lizzie said. "Is that Toby?"

"No, but I want you to meet him. Toby, I mean. Some other time." It was so ridiculous. Marco being mistaken for Toby. "That's the soccer player who kicked the ball at me. He feels guilty so he thinks he has to take me home."

"Wow. He's just . . ." Lizzie trailed off. There weren't words enough to describe Marco. Not in English anyway.

"I know."

She and Lizzie walked slowly toward the car, with Marco's grandmother following closely behind them, cane in hand.

When Marco opened the door for her, Cindy tried to tell him he didn't have to do this, but he insisted. He helped Cindy into the front seat and fastened her seat belt. He brushed against her breast with his arm and she thought she was having a relapse. Her heart sped up, her skin was covered with goose bumps.

Then Marco lifted his grandmother into the tiny rumble seat behind her. Fortunately she was very small. Small but talkative. She kept up a steady stream in Italian while Marco answered her only briefly as he pulled away from the field where he should be kicking goals.

The last thing Cindy saw was Lizzie standing in the grass staring at the car, looking as stunned as if she'd been dropped into an alternate universe. Cindy knew how she felt. Manderley was a strange place. Lizzie might think being whisked off in a sports car by a dashing foreigner happened to her best friend every day.

She told herself it was no big deal riding with Marco in his car. The guy who hit her was giving her a ride home. It was as simple as that. And yet Lizzie was acting like she was Cinderella riding off in the prince's coach to the castle. Nothing could be further from the truth. Could it?

twenty-seven

*Like all the best families, we have our share of eccentricities,
of impetuous and wayward youngsters and of family disagree-
ments.*

—Elizabeth II

"My grandmother thinks you look too thin," Marco explained
after his grandmother had leaned forward to deliver a long
speech into his ear. They were driving down El Camino with
the wind blowing Cindy's hair. She'd never been in a European
sports car before, and she'd probably never be in one again,
especially with the owner's grandmother squeezed in the back
seat, such as it was.

She wished she could enjoy it more, but her head hurt and
she was confused. She wasn't sure if she was confused because
of her injury or if any normal girl be confused under these
circumstances.

Where had his grandmother come from? If he was a prince, was she the queen? Perhaps the Queen Grandmother, if there was such a title? If so, wasn't she more accustomed to riding in a coach than in the backseat of a small car? Why had she come? Had he expected her at the game? From the look on his face, she had to think no.

"I can't help it, I've always been thin," Cindy said.

"You look fine to me, but you know how grandmothers are."

"Not really," Cindy murmured. What wouldn't she give for an overly solicitous grandmother.

"She's worried about you. She wants to make you some pasta with marinara sauce on it."

"That's very kind, but . . ."

"Kind? No one's ever called her kind before," Marco said with a swift glance in the rearview mirror. "Strong, demanding, interfering, difficult. But then you probably have someone like that in your family. What about your grandmother?"

"I . . . I never knew her. My parents are both dead."

He looked at her, his eyes warm and soft with sympathy. "I'm sorry. But who takes care of you?"

Cindy didn't know whether to laugh or cry. She couldn't say no one, or Marco would feel sorry for her. He might even tell his grandmother.

"My stepmother. So I'm not alone. I'm fine. Really."

Marco's grandmother stuck her head between them and seemed to be asking a lot of questions. Marco explained that she wanted to know what they were talking about.

"She hates to be left out," he said. "Which is why she's here. I mean here in America. She was worried about me, so she flew here from Italy by herself a few days ago. First time in an airplane. First time out of Italy. First time out of her town, actually."

"She must really care about you," Cindy said softly. What must it be like to have a grandmother like that?

"I guess she does. I just wish she hadn't come to the game. I lost my concentration, which is why I kicked the ball in the wrong direction, right at you. Poor little thing." Marco reached over to smooth Cindy's hair.

His touch was so gentle she felt weak all over. Good thing she was strapped into her seat or she would have collapsed for the second time that day. No one had called her little since she was three years old. No one had ever made her feel so cared for in a long, long time. Marco had walked away before the end of an important match to take her home, missing a chance to be hoisted off the field to rousing cheers. He was not like any guy she'd ever known.

"I didn't expect to see my *nonna* here. She says she took a taxi. How she found a taxi in the suburb where I live is a mystery. But my grandmother always finds a way to do what she wants. She's called the *sporganza*, the boss of the family."

carol culver

"We'd say the matriarch," Cindy said. "You're lucky she cares so much." What wouldn't she give to have someone, anyone in her life who cared that much about her.

Marco gave her a rueful smile. "Lucky? I never thought of it that way." Then he turned to talk to his grandmother in rapid Italian while he drove skillfully with one hand on the steering wheel. Cindy only interrupted to give directions to her house.

When he pulled up in front of the house, Cindy reached for the door, and Marco grabbed her backpack and her clarinet and came around to open the door for her. She said *"Arrivederci"* to his grandmother, then Marco carried her things up to the front door.

"Will you be all right?" he asked as Cindy took her house keys out of her backpack.

"I'm fine," she assured him. She would be fine if her knees weren't so weak and if her hands would stop shaking enough to get the key in the lock. Something was wrong with her. Was it her head or was it her heart?

"I'm sorry about the game. I hope they didn't lose at the last minute because of your not being there."

"Don't worry. They can't lose. The other team was terrible. Besides, it's just a game."

"Like poker?"

"Like poker." He paused. "Do you play?"

"No. My father did, but it was just for fun, not for money."

144

"For fun," he said thoughtfully. "For me it has always been about the money. Cindy, I have something to ask you . . ."

Her heart stuttered, she felt like she might have a relapse. Then his grandmother leaned on the car horn.

He shook his head and gave her a rueful smile. "Sorry, I've got to go. *Ciao, bella.*"

twenty-eight

Big sisters are the crabgrass in the lawn of life.

—Charles M. Schulz

Alone in the house, enjoying the rare solitude, Cindy took two aspirin for her headache and crawled into bed with her British Literature book and tried to read a short story about an Italian man who was learning how to live. Why couldn't the teacher have chosen something else? Cindy had enough trouble thinking about something besides a certain other Italian and trying to figure out how to live herself.

When her sisters came home, their conversation wafted in from their bedroom.

"Too bad Marco had to leave. We could have lost at the last minute," Brie said.

"Nobody knows who it was that got hit," Lauren said.

"Some klutz who didn't know enough to get out of the way. Bet she didn't even really get hurt. I mean, nobody takes chances like we do. We put ourselves in danger with every stunt and we don't even get a trainer." Cindy heard a large thump as if Brie had kicked her dresser in frustration.

"It's not easy to cheer when you have a lame cheer team like ours. We do all the work, and they stand around shaking their pom-poms thinking they're so great."

"Especially Lynette, she's the worst."

"What about Pam?"

"Second to the worst. Can hardly lift her fat leg."

"I swear, if we don't get elected team captains . . ." Cindy could just see Lauren's lips forming her usual pout.

"We will. We have to. We're seniors. Who else could do it? Not Sandy; she's like borderline ugly." Brie's whiny voice sounded louder than ever.

"Nobody appreciates us, that's the problem."

"We spend more hours practicing on our own than the team does. Than any team does. Because cheering season never ends," Brie said. "Not for us."

"I'm sick of it. The school doesn't appreciate us. We have no trainer, no mats and a bunch of losers to work with. We practice in the corner of the gym or in the hallway."

"It's not fair."

Cindy heard the phone ring, and a moment later Brie banged on her door.

"It's for you, nerd girl," she said, handing Cindy the phone.

"Hello, Cindy, how are you feeling now?" Marco asked.

"Fine, just fine," she said, closing the door, getting back into bed and pulling a blanket over her head so her sisters couldn't hear. She had the creepy feeling that Brie was standing at her door listening.

"My *nonna* is making you a minestrone soup which I will bring you on Monday."

"That's very . . . um . . . nice." She knew Marco didn't believe his grandmother was kind, but she didn't know what else to say. She was making soup for Cindy, a stranger. She blinked back a tear.

"Will you be at school on Monday?" he asked.

"Of course," she said, trying to sound better than she felt. "I'll be at work tomorrow. I have a job too."

"I know you do. But again tomorrow? You Americans are so busy. Don't you ever want to just, how to say, kick something and relax, listen to music or lay in the sun by the pool?"

"You mean kick back? Yes, of course, but not now. I have to get good grades to get into a good college. I have to make money to pay for my education. Besides, I like being busy."

"I see. And after this good college, then what?"

"Then what? I don't know. A job. A real job where the boss is not my stepmother."

"Maybe you'll be the boss someday. You'll be good at it. You'll be a fair boss, very . . . *giusto*."

"You think so? I hope so." How he knew she'd be a fair boss, she had no idea. But Marco had a way of making her feel good about herself.

"I know. Now maybe you can hear in the distance, my *nonna* is calling me. She wants to take care of me. She can't understand I'm too old for that. It's unfortunately just like being home in Italy." She couldn't understand why there was a note of sadness in his voice. It couldn't be because he missed home. He had his grandmother right there. Right now she'd give anything to have a grandmother hovering over her, making soup and taking care of her. Unfortunately she only had a stepmother, with an emphasis on the "step."

"Who was that?" Brie yelled the minute Cindy hung up.

"No one," Cindy said.

"Because it sounded like Marco the Italian exchange student."

"Really?"

"Except why would he be calling you, loser?"

Cindy shrugged, even though Brie couldn't see her through the closed door. Why give her the satisfaction of an answer?

"Was it a wrong number?" Brie said.

"Yeah, that's right," Cindy said.

twenty-nine

On Halloween the thing you must do
Is pretend that nothing can frighten you.
An' if somethin' scares you and you want to run,
Jus' let on like it's Halloween fun.

—Early-nineteenth-century postcard

Cindy felt like an idiot for studying her Italian lessons on tape because she barely saw Marco at all for the next two weeks. So what was the point? Did she have someone to converse with in Italian? Was she going to Italy some day on vacation? Not likely.

Marco said he was too busy for tutoring. He was practicing with the team and coaching a girls' team, and he was supposed to be home (his *nonna*'s orders) at night for dinner. He mentioned in his e-mail that dinner in Italy was at nine or ten o'clock, but still he was feeling the pressure to hang around while his *nonna* was there.

He did deliver a container of delicious soup to her at school and she wrote a thank-you note in Italian to his *nonna*. When he looked at it, he grinned. He had the most contagious smile, so all she could do was to smile helplessly back at him.

"I guess I made some mistakes," she said.

"Just one, you thanked her for the soap, *sapone*, instead of the soup—*minestra*. I didn't know you knew any Italian. I'll have to be careful what I say."

"It's a beautiful language," she said.

"I'll give you a lesson. *Ciao*."

"*Ciao*," she said. "I know that one. It means hello, doesn't it?"

"And good-bye. Also *addio* is good-bye."

"What else?"

"*A presto* for *see you soon*. *Spiacente* means *I'm sorry*. See how easy it is? Some day I will teach you more."

Some day? When was that? Cindy knew better than to ask. She knew that promises didn't always come true. She knew she could only count on herself. No one else. She went back to studying, working in the office and helping out at the spa when she couldn't avoid it.

She also went to her sisters' physics class. They said they had to go to a college information seminar that hour and they told her to go to their class and record the lecture for them. She said she couldn't. She had an SAT practice session sched-uled. But Brie said she and Lauren would fill in for her at the spa on Saturday if Cindy would go to physics. Cindy wanted to know why they couldn't ask a friend in the class to do it, but they said they had no friends in that class. The class was full of dorks and they had no intention of being friends with any of them. That they had no friends there was easy to believe.

So Cindy accepted the bribe and took their tiny handheld tape recorder with the voice-activated microphone and sat in the lab for an hour with the mike turned on while she tuned out.

The physics class was boring. Not like her favorite class— geometry. She loved the problem solving and she got a kick out of Scott, who sat behind her and continued to nag her about a makeover.

"What are you wearing to the Halloween homecoming dance?" he asked as they walked down the steps after class.

"Nothing," Cindy said. "I'm not going."

"Not going? You have to go. Don't you love Halloween? It's my favorite holiday. The costumes, the makeup, the candy. What's not to like?" he asked.

"If you put it that way," she said.

"You haven't even thought about it, have you? You gotta get yourself a dynamite costume and go."

"I don't think so."

"Why not? Your friend Marco is nominated for homecoming king. Don't you want to cast your vote for him?"

"He won't need my vote."

"It should be fun, if the headmaster doesn't put the kibosh on the dancing along with everything else. Costumes are de rigueur." He poked Cindy in the arm. "That means mandatory to you."

"I got that," Cindy said. "Us Castle transfers are not all complete dolts."

"I'm going as Marie Antoinette. What do you think?"

Cindy laughed. "Cross-dressing? You wouldn't. I don't think the new headmaster would approve."

"Screw the new headmaster. Do you know he's trying to shut down the Gay-Lesbian Alliance and any other activity that doesn't meet his morality standards? Besides, who would know who I was if I wore a mask, which I would, and kept muttering 'Let them eat cake.'" He said it in a high falsetto.

Cindy giggled. "Look, Scott, I don't have a costume, and besides, I'm kind of busy that night."

"What are you busy doing, trick-or-treating in your neighborhood? Come on, Cindy. I know, you can wear my Marie Antoinette costume."

"But what would you wear?"

"I'll be Louis the Sixteenth, your consort. I've got the tights and my legs aren't that bad—so I've been told. All I need is a white wig and an ermine cape. Can't you see it?" He flung his arm out in a dramatic gesture and knocked into a student coming up the staircase.

"Flaming queers," the guy muttered.

Cindy froze but Scott kept walking. Either he didn't hear or he didn't care what anyone thought. That was the good thing about Scott, he was completely secure with who he was.

She never thought she'd have a guy friend that could match her BFF, but now she had Scott and Marco too. She wished Marco could be more than a friend, but Cindy was a realist above all else. And she needed all the friends she could get.

"Of course Marie Antoinette didn't have red hair," Scott said, tilting his head to survey her.

"That settles it then, I can't be her so I can't go."

"Yes, you can. We can make your hair chestnut with a temporary rinse. Or a wig. Yeah, maybe a wig." He wrapped his finger around one of her curls and studied it as if he were an artist. Which he was. Cindy had seen some of the drawings of his own fashion creations. She didn't doubt for a minute he could make a fabulous Marie Antoinette costume and that he would be the next Isaac Mizrahi. What she doubted was that she could make a halfway decent queen of France, or of anything.

His eyes sparkled and he beamed a bright smile at her. "You'll need a push-up bra, but I'll do everything else, with some help from my friends. Then it's a date."

"Okay," Cindy said. She couldn't turn him down. He was so excited about it. If only she felt the same. Maybe when he saw her in the dress, he'd realize she couldn't pull it off. Maybe when he tried to make her hair look like Marie's he'd realize it was a hopeless job. Then she could gracefully retreat and spend the night at home alone with a good book, or even a bad book. Anything would be better than subjecting herself to another Manderley dance. Anything would be better than watching Marco dance with someone, then be crowned homecoming king with a gorgeous queen at his side. Someone like one of her sisters, or both of them. She shuddered at the thought.

thirty

War is the only game in which it doesn't pay to have the home-court advantage.

—Dick Motta

When Toby went to Lily Langtry Gardens to pick up his grandfather on the day of the oral report, the nurse said Mr. Hatcher hadn't slept well and wasn't feeling good. Toby's heart sank. He knew this would happen. He'd told Cindy not to count on the old man. He told her they should do a PowerPoint presentation like everyone else. But no, she wouldn't listen to him. She said they'd get a better grade this way. She was some kind of optimist. A pushy optimist.

For one thing, she didn't know his grandfather. He'd heard she was an orphan herself, which must have its advantages. He'd also heard she was gay, but he wasn't sure about that.

She didn't have a special butch girlfriend that he could see, but she did hang out with Scott Hartley, the president of the Gay-Lesbian club, so maybe it was true.

Today he envied her her lack of family, because if it weren't for his grandfather, he wouldn't be here. His grandfather not only didn't know who he was, but he refused to get dressed.

"Gramps," he said, sitting on the edge of the old man's bed. "Get up. You're coming to school with me today."

"School?" His bleary eyes looked past Toby to someplace in the far distance. "Too late. Too late."

"No, it's not too late. It's early. I came early to get you."

"Got a bellyache. Can't go to school today."

Toby nodded. He'd often used that one himself. These days it was his head that hurt. Ever since the night of the Welcome Dance he hadn't had a drink. Was that why his hands were shaking and his head was pounding? At least he wasn't retching.

"Maybe after you have breakfast you'll feel better," Toby said.

"Food's no good. Can't eat it."

"I brought you some coffee and a donut. That'll make you feel better." Toby looked over his shoulder to make sure a nurse wasn't watching or she'd probably snatch it away and insist Gramps eat some kind of lumpy hot cereal and canned orange juice.

Then Toby opened a white paper bag and set the coffee

and the glazed Krispy Kreme donut on the metal tray in front of him. His grandfather's eyes focused for the first time since Toby arrived. He took a big bite out of the donut and chewed noisily. Then he drank some of the Starbucks double latte to which Toby had liberally added cream and finally he looked Toby in the eye.

"That's good," he said. "Who're you and what do you want?"

"I'm Toby, your grandson. I came to take you to school today. We talked about it. You said you'd come to my class," Toby said with a note of desperation. "I'm Jonathan's son, re-member?"

"Jonny's boy? Where is he? Never comes to see me."

"He's busy. He's a doctor." Too busy taking care of the sick to visit his own father. "You're wearing your uniform and you're gonna talk about the war. Everyone wants to hear about it." At least that's what Cindy thought. If she was wrong, he'd be humiliated. If she was right, he might get a good grade on this report.

"What war?"

Uh-oh. Maybe Toby should just cut class today. Cindy could manage by herself. She was a smart girl. For a lesbo she wasn't bad looking. He could say he was sick. Sure, it might be suspicious, getting sick the day of the oral report, but it happened. It would be better than parading his grandfather in front of the class only to have him sit there staring off into space saying *What war?* That was no way to get an A or even a C. That was the path to mass pity and disgust from the class and a rock-bottom grade for the report.

Toby decided to give it one more try. Then he'd phone in sick. He went to his grandfather's closet and pulled out his uniform, stiff and clean with the medals still pinned to the jacket. Toby held it up and there seemed to be a vague light of recognition in the old man's eyes. That was a good sign.

He coaxed his grandfather out of bed with another donut and somehow, though it took about a half hour, Toby got his grandfather dressed except for his shoes. He had to ask the nurse for help to get his feet into the black dress shoes.

"Where are you going?" she asked Toby as she combed his grandfather's hair. "Some kind of veteran's thing?"

"I'm taking him to school with me so he can tell the class about the Second World War," Toby said.

"Oh, like show and tell?"

"Right."

Just then his grandfather straightened his shoulders as if he'd been told to stand at attention, and gave the nurse a sharp salute. "Gonna tell them about Corregidor and Leyte. About how we fought the Japs. I was there when MacArthur told 'em, 'I shall return.' Me too. I shall return," he told her.

Toby exchanged a glance with the nurse. She nodded and helped his grandfather out to Toby's car. In the rearview mirror he could see her standing in front of the redbrick building watching them as they drove away, her hand at her forehead in an unmistakable salute.

His head cleared a little. He smiled to himself. This might turn out okay after all.

thirty-one

Music is your own experience . . . If you don't live it, it won't come out of your horn.

—Charlie Parker

"We'll need several more music acts for the all-school concert," Henderson told the jazz band. "Besides Sam and his quartet, we have Joanie doing a guitar solo. How about a piano piece?"

When Eric's arm shot up, Henderson sighed but he was ready for him. "Eric, you're already playing 'Autumn Leaves,' that's all we can reasonably ask of you, considering . . ." He didn't say considering what, but everyone knew Eric had a fragile ego as well as plenty of other problems. Especially knowing Michelle had once again turned him down for the homecoming dance. Not only that, he hadn't been nominated for homecoming king again this year, though he'd vigorously campaigned for it with posters, stickers and homemade cookies.

"Let's see some spirit here," Henderson begged. "Look, a new music room is on the list of upgrades for next year. We've got to show the administration we need it. We deserve it just as much as we need a new stadium with a retractable roof. Show 'em how we love our music."

"I could play a swing piece," Marco said from the back of the room. All heads swiveled in his direction. He hadn't shown up to jazz band for two weeks. Now he was volunteering to do a solo? "It's my favorite music, your piano player Teddy Wilson, or maybe Jess Stacy, you know?"

Henderson looked around the room. "See that? How does that make you feel? A European import is going to play our great American music for us. Okay, Marco, you're on."

"The problem . . . the problem . . . I have mostly played in trio and quartet at home," Marco said. "I play, how to say, accompaniment, some improviso . . . But I need somebody to play with me. Songs like 'Somebody Loves Me,' 'Sometimes I'm Happy' or 'If I Could Be with You,' something like those, very much favorites in my country."

"Songs like those," Henderson said, his eyes wide, a smile on his face for a change. "That shouldn't be hard. All we need is someone to play Benny's clarinet parts for you." Henderson looked around the room. Cindy held her breath. She wasn't the only clarinet. Why didn't Marco say he wanted her? Because he didn't want her?

Benny Goodman? She couldn't play like Benny Goodman. Only Benny Goodman could do that.

"Don't look at me, Mr. Henderson," Sam said. "I'm used to sticking to the score. Not much of an improviser." His mouth was turned down in a way that suggested playing jazz was beneath his standards.

Cindy dared to glance over at Marco, who was looking directly at her. Why? If he wanted her to be his accompanist, why didn't he say so?

"Cindy," Henderson said. "How about you?"

Cindy felt her face flush and her hands shake. She thought about saying she couldn't do it. She couldn't learn the music in time. Then she heard herself say "Sure, why not?" as if someone else had spoken the words and she'd just moved her lips like a puppet. Who did she think she was, the second coming of Benny Goodman himself?

"Good enough," Henderson said. "Get your horn and meet Marco in the piano room. Remember, it's a *music* room. If I don't hear music coming out of it, I'm coming in." The band members chuckled. There were a few ribald comments, which Cindy pretended she didn't hear as she grabbed her clarinet and scurried out of the room before they noticed how red her face was. Scott gave her a thumbs-up as she passed by his section.

When she got to the music room Marco was already playing some riffs on the piano. She thought about telling him he
was so good he didn't need anyone else (which was true, he
sounded great), but she didn't. If he didn't object to playing
with her, she'd be an idiot to turn him down.

Marco turned as she came in but kept playing softly as he
talked. "I was hoping you would agree to play with me," he
said. "You know more about American swing than I do."

"I'm not sure," she said. "I heard American swing is more
popular in Europe than here. Here the kids think it's old-
fashioned." She opened her case and assembled her instrument.
She chose a new reed and put it into her mouth to moisten it.

"But you are different," he said. "You know the melodies,
I think. They're part of your inheritance, is that the right
word?"

"Heritage. Yes, maybe it is. My father taught them to me,
this is his clarinet he left to me. But don't make me sing the
words."

"As you like. Just the tune. I think Benny Goodman didn't
know words either, yes?"

With that he segued into a fast-paced version of "Sometimes I'm Happy" and Cindy wondered if she'd ever been so
happy herself. Alone in the music room with the sexiest man
alive, the window open to the soft afternoon breeze and the
most romantic swing music in the air. What more could a girl
want?

She blew a few tentative notes, trying not to squeak. A poorly played clarinet could sound shrill and painful to the ears. Her stepsisters used to walk around holding their ears and turning up the radio when her father was teaching her to play. Now they'd slam the door and refuse to let her practice at home.

She soon found the key Marco was playing in and followed him with the melody. After a few false starts she tuned in to the rhythm. Marco's fingers flew across the keyboard. Then he looked up and sent her a smile that said, *Look how we make beautiful music together*. Her heart skipped a few beats but she kept playing.

The encouragement must have gone to her head because a minute later she stumbled and her tempo fell behind, but Marco slowed to let her catch up. They locked glances and Cindy felt a connection, like a cord stretched taut between them, something she'd never felt with anyone before.

She wondered if he felt the same at all. Or if he'd felt this so many times over with his accompanists or with girls in general that it no longer meant much. It didn't matter. It was happening now. And it was happening to her. No one else. Just her.

Cindy picked up the tempo and the volume to match Marco. They played around with the tune for several minutes, then she got brave and did a few ad-lib runs of her own. Some worked, others didn't, but Marco held it together. Just as if they'd been playing like this all their lives.

165

"We're good together," he said with a grin when they finally stopped playing. "I love that music. I want to play you some music I have on CD. Artie Shaw and Woody Herman and Benny Goodman at Carnegie Hall. I learned from them better than anyone how to really swing."

Cindy gripped her clarinet tight in her hand. "I'd love to hear them," she said, feeling dazed by the music, the man and the possibilities of making more and better music. With Marco.

"You and I will listen together and play together and you will see, you will feel, you know, *naturale*."

Naturale? So that's what you called this feeling. This breathless, heady, dizzy feeling. *Naturale*.

"Come here," he said, moving to one side of the piano bench. "I want you to see what I'm doing."

She sat next to him, so close his hip pressed against hers.

"This is how I lead into the arpeggio."

His beautiful, strong fingers caressed the keys while she watched. When he reached for the high notes his hand brushed against her breast. She couldn't breathe. All the air had been sucked from her lungs. Even though she thought she might die of asphyxiation, she wished the song would never end. But it did.

He rested his hands on the keys. "We must do this again," he said with a sideways glance out of his dark eyes. Then he put his arm around her shoulders. He looked deep into her eyes and she felt a shiver go up her spine. He leaned toward her. She closed her eyes. She'd never been kissed before. She never expected to be kissed by someone in the music room, and yet something told her it was going to happen now.

Or it would have happened if the door hadn't opened and Eric hadn't burst in. "Okay, you guys," he said with a knowing smirk as Cindy stumbled to her feet. "Time's up. Henderson wants to know what you're doing in here. What'll you give me not to tell him?"

Marco watched Cindy grab her clarinet and hurry out of the room. He sat staring into space for a long time.

What was this strange excitement he felt? This girl Cindy was not his type. She was tall and a little awkward. She had beautiful hair, but normally he required more than that to be attracted to someone. She was long-legged and skittish like a colt. Yet he'd almost kissed her. Had wanted to kiss her. He still did. He would have if that imbecile hadn't barged in.

Maybe it was the music. Yes, that must be it. They made beautiful music together. With some practice it would get even better. Most girls pretended to like the music he liked. She liked it and she could make it. They could make it together.

thirty-two

Costumes and scenery alone will not attract audiences.

—Anna Held

Cindy had been worried about spending the whole day with Scott and his friends. How would she fit in? Why were they doing this for her? But they'd treated her like she was a doll to be dressed up. One of the guys gave her a pedicure and a manicure; another did her hair, then decided she needed her eyebrows waxed and her face exfoliated.

For once she was on the other side of the day-spa experience and it wasn't all that bad. For once she had some empathy for those vain women she'd looked down her nose at. It was fun to be pampered. She'd have a different perspective when she went back to work.

It was a heady experience she wasn't likely to have again, so after a few nervous moments when the guys looked her over and discussed her hair and skin as if she weren't there, she started to relax and go with the flow. After all, what choice did she have? She wasn't about to run out on them.

But now that she was actually at the country club with all the girls who could afford a real day spa as well as the price of an authentic rented costume, she felt a wave of panic. Who would she hang out with? Who would she dance with? Who would talk to her except for Scott?

"Don't look like that," Scott said.

"How do I look?"

"Like you want to run away."

"Who, me?" She wished her voice were more steady. Ditto her hands as well as her stomach. She'd never run out on Scott, not after all he'd done for her. But if he wasn't there . . .

Maybe that's why he was there, to keep an eye on her. No, he was getting a kick out of the costumes, the atmosphere, the music and the camaraderie of his friends. Cindy's eyes popped at the sexy outfits most of the girls were wearing, like the tiny form-fitting white nurse's uniform, the S and M girl with the lime-colored bob wig and a whip in her hand. It made her Marie Antoinette costume, low-cut as it was, look positively tame.

All the while Scott was observing the other guys. "How do you like the vintage Superman with the long flowing red cape over red trunks?" he muttered. "I bet he spent plenty on that."

"I like your cape better," Cindy assured him. "You made it. It's real."

"Yeah, but will anyone appreciate it?" he asked.

"I will."

He grinned at her and straightened her sleeve. "You look great. Remember to smile."

"On my way to the gallows?"

"You're in your garden, you don't have a clue you're going to lose your head."

"I'll try to remember that," she said, tugging on her neckline, which seemed to be slipping dangerously.

"Leave it," Scott ordered. "You'll be the belle of the ball, as they say. Your prince will be dazzled."

Cindy shot him a quick look. Did he know about her crush on Marco? Or was he just guessing?

thirty-three

Love is like pi, natural, irrational, and very important.

—Lisa Hoffman

Cindy gasped when she looked in the mirror in the bathroom of the Bella Vista Country Club, where the homecoming dance was being held. Who was that creature that stared back at her? The one with her small breasts half falling out of the satin bodice, the big sleeves, the tiny waist, the brown curls and the long-lashed eyes behind the gold mask and the pink cheeks.

She was exhausted after hours of dress fittings, and the full spa treatment. Almost as exhausted as she would have been had she worked at the spa today making other women feel pampered. She'd reminded Brie and Lauren of their promise to work for her, but they said they'd never meant this Saturday.

After all, they needed all day to get ready for the dance themselves. But they'd be sure to do it another Saturday.

Cindy thought she'd run out of excuses to give Irina until she came up with an imaginary root canal. Tomorrow she'd have to appear in the morning with a swollen jaw and a bill from a dentist, but she'd worry about that later. Right now she was worried that no one would dance with her except Scott.

Once again she tugged on the low neckline of her dress so that it covered more of her pale white breasts, then went out to the dance floor. The music from the live band was loud but danceable. If no one asked her to dance, she could at least go out on the terrace and pretend to be interested in the gardens.

Then she saw Marco. Even across the room he was hard to miss, dressed as he was in a dashing pirate costume. She broke into a smile as she admired his disguise—the striped shirt over his broad shoulders, the hat on his dark hair, the patch over one eye and a stuffed parrot on one shoulder.

He caught her eye and smiled back at her. She pressed her gloved hands together and took a deep breath. In a minute he'd crossed the room and was at her side.

"Who are you, *mi bella donna*?" he asked, taking her gloved hand and kissing it.

He didn't recognize her! She couldn't believe it. Her disguise must be better than she thought. "Marie Antoinette," she said in a soft voice.

172

"Of course." He stepped back and let his gaze roam over her body. "I didn't recognize you at first. Would you dance with a commoner?"

Cindy only nodded. Half afraid to trust her voice, half afraid of being discovered, she silently let herself be led to the dance floor. He pulled her close and her knees buckled.

"What's wrong?" he asked, bending down to breathe into her ear.

"It's the corset," she said breathlessly. "I'm not used to it." Not used to being held so close to him she could smell the faint odor of leather and sandalwood and feel the brush of his shadow beard against her skin.

She saw Marco glance down the front of her dress. Thank God for the "plunge" push-up bra she'd allowed Scott to talk her into. Those things accomplished miracles. No one who knew how small her breasts were would ever recognize her.

"I'm surprised, Marie, that you come out in public," he said. "Are you not afraid of losing your head?"

Losing her head? If he held her any tighter she'd lose more than that. "Why?" she asked with what she hoped was a flirtatious smile. "Have you heard any rumors about a revolution or anything?" During the day Scott had given her a crash course in the history of the French Revolution, his favorite period. Now she knew more than a little about the queen's unfortunate demise at the guillotine and what had followed.

"Nothing to worry about," he said, tracing the outline of

her cheek with his thumb. "The Jacobins are not at the door yet; neither is the headmaster. Tell me more about yourself, your life at court. It must be very dull."

"Nothing like the life of a pirate, I'm sure. You know all about me, but I don't even know your name." Cindy was feeling more and more like a queen and less and less like an unpopular and geeky high school junior. It had something to do with the costume, but mostly had to do with the man who was holding her like he'd never let her go.

"Guess," he said, pressing his cheek against hers.

"Blackbeard?"

"Not so famous, but twice as ruthless. I eat little children for lunch and seduce a dozen women before sunset. I am Italian, after all. I have a reputation to think of."

"An Italian pirate, I . . . uh . . . Should I know you?"

"By the end of the evening we will know each other very well, I promise you, your majesty, because I won't let you out of my sight. You are not like these other American girls. So simple, so shallow, so empty in the head."

She flushed under her makeup. "Are you Captain Hook?" she asked in an effort to change the subject.

Marco laughed and Cindy felt the vibration right through her seam-free, label-free, stitch-free bra.

"Captain Hook? No, I said Italian. All right, I will tell you. I am Pescatore. I captured many ships and took many hostages in my time."

"I suppose some were women?" she asked boldly, looking up at him from behind her mask, more and more confident he had no idea who she was.

He chuckled, an evil pirate chuckle. "Many, but none so beautiful as you, your highness. By the way, is your husband, Louis the Sixteenth, with you tonight?" He looked over his shoulder as if Louis might be lurking with a sword in hand.

"Yes," Cindy answered, "but we have an arrangement. He goes his way and I go mine. He only wants me to have a good time. He's the one who gave me this necklace."

Marco fingered the faux diamonds Scott had supplied for Cindy. At least she thought they were faux. With Scott she never knew. He liked gems. He said his mother had a large collection. Marco's fingers were cool against her warm skin.

"Very lovely," he said in a low tone that made Cindy's heart thump erratically. "Let me see, I think I read you were married at fourteen. They say you didn't have sex for six years. That you and your husband were virgins. True?"

"Well . . ."

"But now you are a woman of the world, I should think and eager to make up for lost time."

"Oh, yes, absolutely," Cindy said. "If you saw the movie about me you know I love to have a good time. And there's not much I don't know about sex or whatever."

"Perhaps you could even show a pirate some new tricks."

Cindy gulped. She told herself it was all a game. A play, a

masquerade. Was this flirting? Was this what she'd been missing? "Mmmm," she murmured. Behind the mask she could be whoever she wanted to be. Whoever he wanted her to be. A rich, sexy, desirable queen. Why not?

"Do you know, your highness, that your family has a connection with mine?"

"No, I don't think so," she said. No one in Cindy's family was even one tiny part Italian.

"Your sisters were both married to Italians."

"My sisters?" Not Brie and Lauren, but Marie Antoinette's royal sisters. "Oh, my sisters, yes of course. Nice girls."

"Of course there was no Italy as such in those days, but still one sister married the Prince of Parma. I have been told by my grandmother, who keeps track of these things, that another of your ancestors had an affair with one of mine."

"Really? Your grandmother must have a good memory."

"And she loves to talk. Since she can't speak English she has to talk to me, night and day, endlessly."

"She lives with you?" Cindy asked sweetly.

"She's just visiting. She came to check up on me and make some food for me. I think her checking is almost finished and the freezer is full of marinara sauce, so now she can go home."

They danced some more. Slow dances and fast dances. He swung her around and then he held her close. Cindy, who'd never been a dancer, could have danced all night. Like Eliza

Doolittle. Like Eliza she'd been transformed by Scott, her own Henry Higgins. But she'd fallen in love with Marco, not Scott.

A girl cut in to dance with Marco. Cindy didn't know girls did that. Apparently Manderley girls did. At least they did when Marco was around. He turned her down and said he would dance with her later, but he didn't.

Cindy told Marco her head felt light, lighter than air.

"Like a soufflé?" he asked. "Yes, *mi amor*, you are like a soufflé. A lemon soufflé, tart and sweet at the same time."

Cindy's heart fluttered in her corset. So this was what she'd been missing all these years. Flirting with an Italian. No matter what else happened at Manderley, tonight was worth every penny of the tuition she didn't pay but she would if she could.

The band took a break. A buffet dinner was served. Cindy and Marco went and filled their plates. There were other couples at their table but Cindy didn't know them. She didn't know what she ate either. Or what anyone said. Then they danced some more.

Sometime soon the homecoming king would be crowned. Cindy hoped it wouldn't be Marco. Then he wouldn't be hers anymore. He'd belong to the world. The world of Manderley.

Marco suggested they take a break from the crowded, noisy dance floor. They went outside and stood on the stone terrace of the country club gazing out at the formal gardens. For a while they didn't speak.

Cindy knew she'd never be there again. After all, the membership was exclusive. It was the kind of place Irina would kill to belong to. She'd have to kill, because there was a waiting list, plus an exorbitant initiation fee. It was all make-believe. Her being there tonight in this dress with Marco. At midnight she'd turn back into a high school junior, a part-time spa assistant, and the flirtatious, sexy woman in the queen's costume would be gone forever.

Marco would be the same. Pirate or not, he'd be handsome, dashing, super-confident, sexy and charming. She'd be shy, stiff, skinny, nerdy and unconfident around guys.

They would still be friends. He might teach her some Italian words. He'd still play the duet with her. But he'd never know, never guess, never *believe* she was the same girl he'd danced with tonight.

And she'd never tell him.

Cindy thought no one would know who she was. But she was wrong. Someone knew. Someone who wanted to get rid of her. Not for good. Just for tonight. And that someone did.

thirty-four

All I say is kings is kings, and you've got to make allowances.
Take them all around, they're a mighty ornery lot. It's the way
they're raised.

—Mark Twain

When Marco was announced as the winner of the homecoming king crown, the whole room erupted into cheers.

He grinned at Cindy and squeezed her hand.

"What do you say, will you be my queen?" he asked.

Cindy nodded. But deep inside she knew it couldn't be. It was all a dream. Her, Cindy Ellis, homecoming queen? In a minute Marco would look at her, really look at her, and he'd see not a glamorous, tricked-up, decked-out eighteenth-century queen, but rather an ordinary teenager. Not even ordinary. Downright plain. And he'd drop her as a romantic interest as fast as he'd picked her up. It didn't matter. She'd always have tonight. And he'd always be her friend. That would have to be enough.

"I'll be right back," Marco said. Then he went to the bandstand to accept his award and he left Cindy's side for the first time that evening.

Cindy's cell phone beeped. She pulled it out of the tiny pocket hidden under the voluminous fabric of her skirt and listened to her voice mail.

"Cindy, where are you? Your stepmother had a heart attack. She needs you. Come home right away."

Cindy didn't know who'd called. She had no time to think. She ran out to the driveway and begged one of the waiting limo chauffeurs to drive her home. A heart attack? She remembered when her father had his. It was a massive coronary and she'd barely had time to say good-bye before he died in the cold, impersonal hospital room. It would be different with Irina of course. How do you say good-bye to someone you don't like?

Marco was crowned king in front of his classmates, who whooped and cheered as if they'd known him for years. He said a few words about how happy he was to be at Manderley, at homecoming and in America, then the band started playing again and he hurried back to find Cindy so they could continue dancing and having fun. But she was nowhere to be found.

He did find her sisters, the two blond girls with bland faces who wore too much makeup and laughed too much.

They didn't see him come up behind them.

"Can you believe that was her?"

"It had to be. Who else is that tall and that geeky and would wear that ridiculous costume?"

"But dancing with Marco? I don't get it."

"I know. You know he plays poker. Well I bet one of his poker dudes bet him he couldn't spend all evening with her. So he did. Just to win the bet. Why else?"

"You're right. Why else?"

Marco only understood half of what they were saying before he butted in. "Where's Cindy?" he asked.

"Who?"

"Your sister. Marie Antoinette."

They stared at him blankly. "Oh, Cindy," Brie said after a brief silence. "She was bored so she left early. That's Cindy. She's weird. She got a ride home from some guy she knows. Said to tell you to have a good time and good luck."

Marco frowned. Good luck? Cindy was bored? Cindy left without saying anything? With some other guy? He thought they were having a good time pretending he didn't know who she was and flirting with her. He *was* having a good time. The best time of his life.

Cindy's sisters grabbed him and made him do one of those

ridiculous line dances. He couldn't refuse without being rude, but he was no longer having a good time.

When he finally got away he could hear them talking about Cindy again, but he'd heard enough.

Riding in the limo toward her house Cindy felt guilty even thinking about Irina dying. Maybe it was her fault for not being nicer to her stepmother. Maybe she'd sensed Cindy's hostile thoughts. When Cindy got out of the limo she saw the house was dark. Had Irina already died? Been taken to the hospital? She ran into the house and up the stairs, her dress dragging behind her, her wig askew, her mask hanging by a cord around her neck.

When she opened the door to Irina's room, her stepmother sat up in bed and screamed.

"Oh my God, Cindy, you scared the shit out of me! What do you want?"

"Are you all right?"

"I was until you woke me." She switched on her bedside light. "What's that you're wearing? You look ridiculous."

"You mean you didn't have a heart attack?"

"If I had, you would have been responsible, bursting in here like that." She snapped off the light. "Get out."

*   *   *

Marco couldn't believe Cindy would have just walked out when he'd told her he'd be right back. She was always fun to tease and nice to look at. But until tonight he hadn't realized she was really beautiful. Oh, he knew she was smart. He knew she was musical and good at math, and he knew she was sweet and shy. But he didn't know how right she'd feel in his arms and how much he'd want her there again.

Had she really been so bored she'd left with someone else? In Italy that would be grounds for a duel. Or it would have been in his grandfather's day. He stood in the parking lot, the cardboard crown perched crookedly on his head, asking himself why he'd let her go even for a few minutes. Did she know who he was? Did she know *he* knew who *she* was?

He paced back and forth restlessly, then he walked out to where the chauffeurs were waiting in limos. He asked one of them if they'd seen Cindy. They said a girl had asked for a ride home about a half hour ago. She'd dropped her cell phone. The chauffeur held it out. Marco said he'd take it to her.

First he played back her old messages. Her stepmother was sick. No wonder she'd left. But why didn't she tell him? He would have driven her home. He got into his car and drove to her house. He had the address from the school Facebook. There it was under her picture, which wasn't at all the way she really looked.

He knocked on her front door. Nothing. No one. Where had she gone? To the hospital?

"Cindy, are you in there?" he shouted. Silence.

Frustrated, he pounded on the front door. Still nothing. He stood staring at the dark house, willing someone to answer. A moment later the front porch light came on. A woman in a robe trimmed with faux fur opened the door and glared at him. "Who are you and what do you want?"

"Is Cindy home from the dance?"

"Dance? Cindy doesn't go to dances. Of course she's home. Now get out of here before I call the police."

The woman tried to close the door in his face. He couldn't really blame her for being suspicious of a pirate with a crown on his head and a funny accent. He braced his hand against the door.

"She lost her phone. Would you give it to her?"

The woman snatched the phone and slammed the door. Marco stood there for a long moment, then he turned and went to his car. He drove home slowly, thinking of Cindy, the girl who tutored him in English, the girl who played the clarinet and made beautiful music with him, and the girl who'd danced all night with him. This wasn't the way the evening was supposed to end.

Cindy had gone home without him because her stepmother was sick. But she didn't look sick to him. Maybe she really had left because she was bored. If she was, he was going to have to be a lot more fun to be with or he'd lose her. He didn't want to lose her; not when he'd just found her.

When he arrived back at his aunt and uncle's estate, lights were blazing from every window.

Inside his grandmother was sitting in a chair by the fireplace, her suitcase at her side.

"I'm leaving," she said in Italian.

"Now?" He ran his hand through his hair. His crown fell to the floor.

"As soon as you drive me to the airport."

"*Nonna*, I've had a bad night and I just got here. Can't you wait until tomorrow? What's the rush? I thought you wanted to take care of me."

She pursed her lips. "You can take care of yourself now. I can see that."

"Wait, I need your advice."

She raised her eyebrows in surprise. "Finally, my grandson needs my advice," she said. "Very well, sit down."

"Is it possible to fall in love in one night?" he asked.

"Of course. It happens all the time. I fell in love on my sixteenth birthday."

"With *Nonno*?"

"No, it was someone else. He left the next day to fight in the war. I married your grandfather instead. I've always wondered what happened to Luigi."

Marco put his head in his hands. He was in no mood to talk about missed opportunities or lost love. "But I thought . . ."

"Who is the lucky girl? Is it the one with the red hair?" She clicked her tongue against the roof of her mouth. "I'd like to take her home with me and feed her some decent Italian food."

Marco managed a half smile. "Yes, it's her. But she ran out on me tonight."

"No one runs out on my grandson," she said, shaking her fist at anyone who would dare. "Don't just sit there, do something. *Chi dorme non piglia pesci.*"

"He who sleeps doesn't catch fishes," Marco muttered. "In other words, I'm not supposed to sleep?"

"Not now. Go to her house. Tell her you love her."

"*Nonna*, we're not in Italy anymore. People don't do things like that here."

"Then you come home with me. You and your girlfriend. *Chi lascia la strada vecchia per la nuova sa quel che lascia, ma non sa quel che trova.*"

"She's not my girlfriend. Not yet. And I can't go anywhere. Not until I talk to her."

"Go call her then. I'll make you something to eat. You look hungry."

"I'm not hungry, I'm confused."

"It's the same thing," she said.

"Cindy." Marco left a message when she didn't answer her

phone. "I knew all the time it was you at the dance. But did you know it was me, Marco? I found your phone and brought it to your house, but your stepmother wouldn't let me in. Please call me and tell me you're okay. And tell me how you feel . . . about me. About everything."

thirty-five

Don't get mad, get even.

—Robert F. Kennedy

Cindy didn't call Marco that night. She didn't trust herself to stay calm. She was afraid she might cry or scream. She felt so stupid. She'd believed whoever it was who had called her. She'd run out on Marco for no good reason. He wanted to know if she was okay. She wasn't.

When her sisters came home, she had to listen to their voices that carried through the walls as they rehashed the dance and dissed everyone—their costumes, their dancing, their dates and their attitudes, especially their friends and fellow cheerleaders. Did they know she'd been at the dance? Did they care? Probably not, unless they were the ones . . . No, they were cruel, but not that cruel.

She was just reaching for her earplugs so she could block out their voices when she heard them mention her name. She knew she shouldn't listen. She knew it would just hurt her, but she couldn't help it. She pressed her ear against the wall.

"She looked so bizarre. Oh my God, I couldn't believe that costume."

"He looked relieved when she left."

"Marco? For sure. Finally he got to have some fun once she was gone."

Cindy had heard enough. She stuffed her earplugs in her ears and let the tears flow. Had Marco really been relieved that she had left?

On Sunday she went to take the costume back to Scott. On her way she walked up and down the winding suburban streets, past the huge mansions and the sprawling estates, and she wiped away the tears that trickled down her cheeks.

She wasn't crying because she was in love with a guy who didn't love her. He'd said he liked her a lot. He knew who she was and he'd flirted with her. That should be enough to make her happy.

She wasn't crying because her sisters hated her. She'd known that for a long time. She was crying because, well, just because she felt like it. Once she got it out of her system, she'd be fine.

She had to pull herself together. First she had to apologize to Marco, then find out who'd called her.

Scott told her she'd looked fabulous. She and Marco looked gorgeous together. He took some credit for it, but he was so proud of her and of himself she didn't begrudge him one bit of the credit he deserved.

"Why did you take off so soon?" he asked.

"I . . . It's a long story. There was a family emergency. At least, that's what I thought."

"Your mean, slutty sisters are the family emergency," he said. "What is it with them? If I were you I'd avoid them like the plague. Yeah, maybe that's their problem. They've got the plague and they oughtta be quarantined. As soon as you left they were all over Marco like glue. Dancing. Flirting."

She shouldn't have been surprised. They were obsessed with Marco. The surprising thing was they'd waited until she left to make their move. Why hadn't they just cut in on them? It wasn't because they were too shy.

"Did they have something to do with your so-called family emergency?"

"Oh I doubt it. The funny thing was that I got the message and not them, because it was about their mother."

"What are you gonna do about them?" he asked, his gaze so sympathetic and so kind she felt like crying again.

"What I always do. Ignore them," she said.

After she left Scott's she stopped and leaned against a tree and played back her voice mail, including the message she got that night. Listening closely, she realized it was Brie's voice. Brie telling her to go home. But why? Irina wasn't sick. A wave of anger hit her fully in the chest and almost knocked her over. They'd done it to get rid of her. On purpose. How could they stoop so low? They'd gone too far this time. Somehow, some way, she would get back at them.

On Monday she was feeling much better and stronger. She looked for Marco but she didn't see him at school. She heard someone say he'd gone back to Italy. Maybe he'd never come back. And she'd never get a chance to explain why she'd left the dance. A tear trickled down her cheek. Impatiently she brushed it away. Self-pity would get her nowhere.

Brie and Lauren came up to Cindy at lunch. Cindy almost choked on her sandwich. They must have been desperate if they'd consider talking to her at school where their friends might see them with her and wonder. They obviously had no clue she knew what they did.

"We need you to record another lecture for us at two o'clock," Brie said.

"No."

They didn't seem to hear her. "This time make sure the

carol culver

switch is in the VOX position. That way it only records when it hears a voice, and we can get more lectures on it before it fills up. Get it right this time."

"I'm not going to, Brie."

"You have to see 'VOX' and 'Recording' on the screen or you won't be recording. After the lecture, press Stop." Brie plunked the small handheld recorder on the table in front of Cindy.

"I know how to do it. I did it before."

"Then what are you looking at me in that brainless way for? How hard can it be?"

Cindy took a deep breath. It was time to take a stand. To be a rebel. At least, take the first step toward being one.

"It's not hard, but I can't do it this time," she said.

"Of course you can. You have to because we're busy at two. Then at three we need you to put on the music for our cheer-leading practice. Here's the CD. We'll be in the gym and it will only take a minute. You know the sound booth on the second level? Go there, put the music in and turn up the volume, then you can go do whatever lame thing you do. After practice we'll be voting on the new team captains. We *have* to be team captains, do you understand that?" Lauren said. "It's our right. We earned it, we deserve it. If we don't we won't get a scholarship to UCLA."

"Are you saying if you mess this up, you'll be screwed?" Cindy asked thoughtfully.

192

"Well finally someone is catching on," Brie said, rolling her eyes at Cindy's stupidity. "This is important, Orphan Girl, so pay attention."

Cindy nodded, but her mind was working double time. The words were running through her head. *Screw up, pay attention, we won't get the scholarship . . .*

She liked working in the dean's office after lunch when it was quiet, and she had mindless work to do so she could think. Today she was thinking of her sisters and how they had used her, how they'd played the meanest trick in the world on her and she'd fallen for it. They'd ruined her magic evening and now they expected her to help them get what they wanted.

She set her backpack down and the twins' dictation machine fell out. When she picked it up, she noticed the Recording icon was flashing. Maybe she'd forgotten to stop the machine after that last lecture.

Uh-oh, she thought, *since it's voice-activated it's been recording everything since the lecture*. Brie and Lauren weren't going to be happy about this. She really didn't care much about their happiness, but she'd erase it anyway and they'd never know. She pressed the Rewind button and a girl's voice came out. It was Lauren talking to Brie.

"Wish I'd seen Cindy's face when she got the message."
Laughter.

"Can't believe she fell for it."

"Serves her right, falling all over poor Marco. He's too hot to even be in her league."

"Thought we didn't know who she was. Hah!"

Cindy felt cold all over. Yes, intellectually she knew it was them. But she hadn't known how gleeful they were, how hateful they were, until she heard their actual voices. Her stomach heaved.

There was no denying they'd used their own mother as bait to get Cindy to leave the dance.

But why? Jealousy? Jealous, of her? Because she was dancing with Marco? She shook her head in disbelief.

They did it to her. They knew how gullible she was, how naïve. And they'd loved doing it. They were proud of themselves. She could hear it in their voices. What was wrong with her for not striking back immediately? No more. That was it. She'd had it.

She should have turned the machine off before she heard any more, but she couldn't. She felt a sick compulsion to keep listening. Soon they tired of talking about her and switched the subject to their fellow cheerleaders.

Cindy's ears burned at their language. Everything they'd ever said about the team—and that was plenty—was tame compared to this. They really let loose this time. Names, descriptions of their butt-ugly faces, their lumpy, clunky bodies, their dumpy gymnastic mistakes, and their clumsy moves were all documented in Brie and Lauren's most colorful language.

"You know what?" Cindy said to herself. "This is crap and I'm not taking it anymore."

By three Cindy's adrenaline was flowing like wine and she felt about a thousand times better. More sure of herself. More determined to get even. She walked briskly across campus to the gym. She made her way quietly up to the sound booth at the top of the bleachers. The sound system was already on, its green lights glowing. She inserted the CDs into the two players and found the volume controls on the master panel.

Why was she doing this? She didn't have to. She could say she just forgot. But that wasn't enough. That was a cop-out. Whatever she did to them, she wanted them to know she'd done it on purpose. They thought she was just good old Cindy. She wasn't. She was a new Cindy, and she was mad as hell.

She looked down into the gym. A girl named Pam, who was totally dissed on the tape, waved to her and shouted to start the music. If only Pam knew what her sisters thought about her "fat ass" and her "nappy" hair. Ditto poor Lynette, who was practicing a backflip on a mat and had no idea what names Brie and Lauren had called her. Not to mention Lisa, who'd messed up their pyramid last week, which made her eligible for the twins' wrath.

Cindy reached for the microphone and pressed a button on the base. "Which CD do you want to hear first?" she asked.

Pam cupped her ears. Cindy pressed another button and said, "Testing, one, two, three." Her amplified voice bounced off the walls of the gym. Pam nodded enthusiastically and gave Cindy a thumbs-up.

Cindy stared down at the girls in their tiny flared skirts and bare midriffs for a long moment. Then she reached into her backpack and found the dictation microphone with her sisters' conversation on it. She propped it up against the sound booth microphone and pressed the Play button.

She didn't stay around to watch the reaction of the cheerleaders. She pictured the faces of the girls as her sisters' voices blasted out so loud no one within fifty yards could ignore them. She imagined shock and disbelief and finally fury as they realized what Brie and Lauren thought of them. She pictured Brie and Lauren running up to the sound booth, frantically trying to turn off the machine. But it would be too late. Way too late.

Cindy left the crime scene as their recorded voices echoed through the gym, the volume up as high as it would go. She knew she was guilty of ruining her sisters' chances of being team captains, and maybe even more. And she didn't even care. In fact, she was brimming over with a kind of satisfaction she'd never known before.

thirty-six

A good love is delicious. You can't get enough too soon. It makes you so crazy, you want to swallow the moon.

—Venus de Milo

It was true. Marco had gone back to Italy. The next time she worked in the dean's office Cindy heard he'd been granted an excused absence from school. For how long, no one knew. She tried to call him but there was just a recorded message on his phone. She told herself it didn't matter that he hadn't said good-bye. It didn't matter that she'd never love anyone again.

It didn't matter that her sisters were furious with her for ruining their lives. They didn't believe she'd done it on purpose even though she didn't deny it. They thought she'd just royally screwed up by playing the wrong recording. Either way she was to blame for what happened. Though really, was it her fault the headmaster canceled all cheerleading activities for the year because he found their outfits to be too revealing and their actions sinful? They thought so.

Brie and Lauren then demanded that Cindy help them write new college essays that didn't have to do with cheerleading. For once in her life Cindy flat-out refused.

"I wouldn't know what to write about for you," she said. "It's too bad about cheerleading. That was *such* a great subject. I can say that even though I'm the one who suggested it to you."

"Yeah," Brie said morosely.

"You could write about how much you miss cheerleading," Cindy suggested. "And the friendship of your peers."

"Who?"

"The other girls. You could say what a loss it is not only for you but for the whole school."

"That's not a bad idea," Lauren said. "You write it, Brie."

"No you. I've already done your Spanish homework for you."

"Hey, what's going on?" Lauren asked as they sat in their jeep in the parking lot. "No one's moving."

"Oh, right," Cindy said. "Didn't you hear? They're having a drug check." Of course they didn't hear. None of the students did. It was hush-hush. An undercover sting, as the headmaster called it. Otherwise all the kids would have hidden their drugs or left them at home. But Cindy'd seen the memo to the teachers while working in the office yesterday.

"What? Why didn't you tell us?" Brie demanded.

"Then you would have dumped your stash. I think using drugs is wrong," Cindy said in her best goody-goody voice, which she knew they'd hate. "Anyone who does it should be punished. Don't you agree?"

They stared at her as if she'd turned into a zombie and was threatening to take a chunk out of their flesh.

"And anybody who lies about their mother having a heart attack deserves whatever they get, right?" Cindy continued with a cool smile.

"Wait. We can explain," Lauren said, facing Cindy from the front seat. "That was a joke. That's all. Tell us what you want. We'll do anything you want. Don't leave us here. We'll be busted."

"Probably. But it's too late. Too late for you but not for me. You know what time it is? It's payback time." Cindy opened the car door and grabbed her backpack. "See you," she said.

"Cindy," Brie shrieked, leaning out the window. "Get back in here. You owe us. You've got to get us through this."

"I don't think so," Cindy called over her shoulder. She couldn't help smiling to herself as she wended her way through the line of cars waiting to exit the lot.

"Open your backpack," the headmaster said. He'd decided this drug check was important enough to take charge himself, with the help of his newly deputized campus monitors who would earn beaucoup points for this operation. After the way he'd cleaned up the dance, he felt empowered.

199

Not as empowered as Cindy felt zipping up her pack. She glanced back at her sisters' jeep, noted with quiet satisfaction the panicked expressions on their faces and walked out past the stone gates. They had reason to panic. The penalty for drug possession on campus was suspension or total expulsion.

Cindy didn't know where she was going. She knew where she was supposed to be going—to Irina's salon to work. She could walk there, but it would take an hour at least and her backpack was already weighing heavily on her shoulders.

She heard a car horn, a high-pitched multitoned sound that could only come from one car. An imported Italian sports car. It was Marco. This time she didn't wave. But he waved at her. Her heart stopped beating. He smiled broadly, pulled over and opened the door for her. "Get in," he said. *"Andiamo!"*

Cindy lost her voice completely. She had a million questions to ask but all she could do was stare at him. At that gorgeous profile, the shadow of a beard on his jaw, the dark hair that brushed the collar of his jacket and the strong hands on the wheel. She drank him in as if he were a glass of delicious Italian soda.

"Where are you going?" he asked.

She shrugged. She wanted to say "anywhere you want," but she didn't. She should have said "to work," but she didn't say that either. Today she was a rebel. Maybe she'd be one tomorrow too. One day at a time.

Marco nodded as if he understood and then he drove

around the block twice. He explained he had a touch of jet lag. He finally parked behind the deserted soccer field. Soccer season was over. Manderley had been eliminated. Without Marco, they were lost.

Without Marco she thought she'd be lost. But she wasn't. She'd been okay without him. With him she was soaring, weightless and giddy.

"I thought maybe you'd gone back to Italy for good," Cindy said finally.

He turned to face her, his arm on the back of her seat.

"No, of course not. I had to take my *nonna* home, but as soon as I could get a place on the plane I hurried back and I'm coming first to see you. You didn't think I would leave forever without saying good-bye?" He gave her an incredulous look.

"No. I mean yes. I didn't know." She wasn't making sense. She was delirious. Marco was back. He'd come first to see her.

"I'm afraid I'm acting not myself. I've forgotten how to speak English," he said. "And I have so much to say to you and no words to say it. And you have explanations to give me, no?"

"Yes, I guess I do. The reason I left the dance was . . ."

"I know that. I heard the message on your phone. Who was that? Is your mother all right?"

"She's fine. She was never sick. It was just someone who wanted to play a joke on me."

"Not a funny joke," he said soberly.

"No."

"I will never understand Americans. You, for example."

"I'm easy to understand," she said, turning to face him.

"I don't think so," he said. "You covered your beautiful red hair for the dance." He wound a long red curl around his finger to admire it with a smile and half-closed eyes. Either he did have jet lag or it was just his usual sleepy, sexy look. "Why?"

"To look like Marie Antoinette. I thought it worked. I thought no one knew who I was."

"I knew. I knew always it was you. No one else talks to me like you do. No one else makes me smile. No one else helps me understand this country and the language and the people who live here." He leaned forward and looked deep into her eyes for a long moment. A look so intense it made her toes curl. Then he drew his eyebrows together. "What I don't know is whether you are my best friend or my girlfriend?"

Cindy stared into his dark eyes with their flecks of green, searching for the right answer. She'd had best friends in the past. She'd have more in the future. But she'd never been anyone's girlfriend.

"Maybe this will help to decide." He leaned forward and kissed Cindy on the lips. His mouth was warm and he tasted dark and delicious. Her lips trembled. Her heart pounded. The least she could do was to kiss him back. Her first kiss. Her first boyfriend. Forever? Who knew? For now? For sure.

After a long, magical moment, Marco broke the kiss. He

brushed a curl from Cindy's cheek. "I am forgetting. My *nonna* sends you a message. She wishes you to visit us in Bellagio next summer. If you are free."

Cindy swallowed hard. She wanted to say yes. She wanted to thank him and his grandmother. But the words stuck in her throat, happy tears filled her eyes and all she could do was nod her head.

Then she realized that although she was free, the airfare wasn't. Never mind, she'd worry about that later. She'd have a bake sale. Whatever. Think about it. All this and Bellagio too.

And now a special preview of the next
book in the BFF series . . .

Rich Girl
A BFF Novel

Coming from Berkley JAM
January 2008!!!

one

"'It was the best of times, it was the worst of times.'"

Victoria Lee read the first sentence of *A Tale of Two Cities* over for the fourth time before it penetrated her tired brain. For her it *was* the best of times, considering her parents had finally left that morning. After spending two weeks with her at their suburban San Francisco McMansion, they were on their way back to Hong Kong.

On the other hand it was also the worst of times. Second semester of her junior year at Manderley Prep, the school where the progeny of Silicon Valley's movers and shakers went, *if* they could pass the stringent entrance exam or *if* their parents do-

207

nated a new stadium or at least a new state-of-the-art theater. Her old friends were left far behind, she had a huge Dickens novel to read, and not much of a new social life in California.

Instead of reading any further, Victoria got out her case of cedarwood colored pencils and sketched the outline of a dress on a blank page in her notebook. In less than a minute she was more engrossed in getting the lines of the slouchy sweater dress right than she could ever be in any old nineteenth-century novel. Now, if that novel had pictures of nineteenth-century fashions, that would be another matter.

"Homework already? The semester hasn't even started."

It was Cindy, her best friend at Manderley—her only friend really—who'd joined her on the second floor of the T. J. Ransom Memorial Library.

Victoria shoved her notebook aside. "Just fooling around, wasting time." That's what her parents would say. *Wasting time drawing clothes. Fashion design? Just what the world needs, another designer making clothes no real woman in her right mind would wear.* That was the point. She would design clothes for real women.

"Good vacation?" Cindy asked, setting her backpack on the corner table.

Victoria sighed. "What vacation? My parents came to town and I never had a chance to catch my breath. When I wasn't chauffeuring them to business meetings in Silicon Valley, they were dragging me to the art museums in San Francisco."

"I thought you liked art."

"Not the kind they like. They love the Palace of the Legion of Honor with all those old European pictures. Portraits of fat rich women stuffed into satin dresses and the stiffs they married standing next to them. I wanted to go to the MOMA with the cool abstract paintings. But no. Next it was, what else? The Asian Art Museum. As if they couldn't get their fill of Asian art in Hong Kong. I went to a coffee shop and tried to read my book there while they insisted I was denying my heritage. What heritage? I said, 'I've got two.' In case they forgot. Of course we had to stop in Chinatown for a tour of a fortune cookie factory."

"You can't get fortune cookies in Hong Kong?"

"Would you believe fortune cookies are a San Francisco invention?"

"Like Rice-A-Roni?"

"I guess so." Victoria reached into the Vuitton Murakami bag she got for Christmas the year before, pulled out a cellophane-wrapped fortune cookie and handed it to Cindy. "We came back with a half-gallon carton of cookies. This one's for you. You'll see why. Go ahead, open it."

"Mmmm, this looks good. They make chocolate-dipped fortune cookies?"

"Chocolate, coconut, strawberry, traditional, jumbo and everything in between. You name it, they make it. We saw the whole thing because the owers are friends of my parents. The assembly line, the chocolate vats, everything. They do special fortunes for showers, parties, weddings or whatever, with fortunes like, 'He loves me, he loves me not. He loves me, we tied the knot.' "

Victoria wrinkled her nose at this sappy verse. If she ever got married, she'd avoid both the sticky sentiment and the cookie factory.

Cindy opened her cookie and read the fortune. " 'You will get 2400 on your SATs and travel across a great ocean.' " Her face lit up. "Hey, do these come true?"

"Guaranteed or your money back," Victoria said. "I thought you'd like that."

"What's in your future this semester?" Cindy asked as she bit into her cookie.

"Right now all I want is a nap. I dropped my parents at the airport this morning at six. I'm so tired I can barely keep my eyes open. Especially when I'm trying to read *A Tale of Two Cities* for Brit lit." Victoria held up her book. "It's got about a thousand pages."

"But don't you see?" Cindy said eagerly, brushing the cookie crumbs off her sweater. "This could be your story. Your life. A tale of two cities. Your mom's city, Hong Kong, and your dad's city, San Francisco."

Victoria thumbed through the book. "Is that what it's about?" she asked hopefully. Cindy would know. She was so smart. And the best part was she didn't act like she knew everything. Rare for Manderley.

"Not really. Those cities are London and Paris, and the year is 1775, but it's really a good book once you get into it."

"I can't get into it. I've tried, and look, I'm still on page one. Honestly they should sell it as an alternative to Ambien. Non-habit-forming and guaranteed to work. Every time I pick it up I feel my eyes getting heavy. I need help, like SparkNotes or watching the movie. Something." If only she could study with Steve, who she knew was going to be in her class this semester. Not that he was so smart, but it would give her an excuse to get together with him.

"I can help you. I read it last year. Hey, you look great," Cindy said, leaning back in her chair. "Cute jumper. So you had time for some shopping over the vacation."

Victoria blushed, happy that someone noticed. She should be satisfied knowing she felt good in what she wore, but having somebody like Cindy notice, someone who didn't normally pay attention to her clothes or anyone else's, was especially sweet. "I made it. Not the shoes though or the leggings."

"Really? I can't believe it. Your parents must be so proud of you."

"Not exactly. They think sewing is a giant time-sucker. In Hong Kong you can have a tailor make you a suit for fifty dollars. Not to mention all the stores there. They always remind me I can hop on a ferry for Tsim Sha Tsui and shop for bargains at the I.T. Sale Shop. They don't see why I should bother making my own clothes."

"Why do you?"

"Everything in the stores is trendy and disposable. Or it doesn't fit. I know what I want but nobody's designed it yet. Besides, I love the whole process, from drawing the pattern to cutting the fabric and then fitting and wearing it. There's nothing like that feeling of doing it all myself."

"You're amazing. Nobody else I know makes her own clothes and lives on her own too. Your parents must really trust you. A lot of kids would go wild and have parties nonstop if they didn't have their parents around breathing down their necks."

"I'd like to have a party but I don't have any friends to invite. The reason my parents left me here is all about the business," Victoria explained. "They bought the house so they could have a residence here. Someone has to live in it and that's me. As a bonus I get to go to Manderley, which should get me into UC Berkeley." Victoria's weak smile turned into a frown. "At least that's the plan." She didn't say that it wasn't *her* plan.

Living alone certainly had its advantages. No parents around telling her what to do. A feeling of freedom that was sometimes scary but mostly exhilarating. Of course they e-mailed her all the time, but that was different. When she first came to California, Victoria had been so homesick without her best friends she begged her parents to let her come back. Of course they said no. Cindy had helped her get over it just by being her first Manderley friend.

"Actually, when my parents were here they hired a house-keeper and now she lives in the apartment above the garage. She's supposed to keep the house clean, do the laundry and oversee the grounds."

"What about you, is she supposed to oversee you too?"

"If she tries, I'll have to set her straight. I've gotten used to my independence and in the past two weeks I've had enough advice and orders to last me years. I tell you it was a shock after being on my own."

"Did you see Steve over the break?"

Victoria shook her head. She'd really missed him. If you can miss someone you hardly ever saw but really, really liked. Steve Heller was the ultimate all-American boy. Blond, blue-eyed, buff and gorgeous. *And* he was studying Chinese. *And* his father was a well-known lawyer in Silicon Valley who made lucrative deals with China for his clients. *And* last but definitely not least, Steve was the star of the basketball team. Victoria hadn't missed a single game.

He wasn't exactly her boyfriend the way Marco was Cindy's, but she thought he liked her. She knew she liked him. Who wouldn't? He was the epitome of the uber California guy. Cindy said they made a great-looking couple. He didn't have another girlfriend, from what she knew. Maybe when basketball season was over he'd have time for a girlfriend. She just hoped it would be her.

"I thought about calling him," Victoria said.

"Didn't you read that book about how to tell if he's not that into you?"

"If it's not on the required reading list, I haven't read it."

"It should be. Here's how it goes: If you haven't heard from him, he's just not that into you."

"What if he's too busy to call me?"

"Those who know say there's no such thing. When men want you, even if they've got homework, college counseling, SAT prep, football practice, yoga, or Tae Kwon Do, they'll find time to make their move, and they do the work."

"I guess maybe he just wants to be friends," Victoria said with a sigh.

"He took you to the Welcome Dance, didn't he?"

"But that was our one and only date. Anyway, he's been away so I didn't expect to hear from him. He told me he was going skiing in Tahoe with his family for the whole vacation," Victoria said. "Maybe there's no cell phone service in the mountains."

"Hmm, maybe. I thought . . . no, I guess not."

"What?"

"I thought I saw his mother come in to the spa last week for a facial when I was working. Maybe she got tired of schussing down the slopes and needed to get rid of her sun spots. Anyway, are you going to be Steve's tutor again this semester?"

"I hope so. I don't know if he'll still need me. He may drop Chinese this semester."

"That doesn't mean he'll drop you. If he likes you he'll think of a way to see you."

"We're going to be in the same English class this semester so I'm bound to run into him, but I can't be his English tutor. Not if I can't read the book."

"There are other subjects you could tutor him in, if you know what I mean," Cindy said with a gentle nudge.

Victoria dropped her pencil and shot a quizzical glance at her friend. "You don't mean sex, do you?" She glanced over her shoulder to make sure they were alone in that part of the library. Just the subject she was dying to broach but was afraid to bring up herself. "If anyone needs lessons in sex ed, which we didn't have at my school, it's me. And soon. I've been very protected."

"Wait, you were Miss Junior Hong Kong. You must have had guys falling all over you so you could have your pick."

"Yes, but they were all either dorky or too smooth. Besides my mother was always watching me like a peregrine falcon."

"Isn't that an endangered species?"

"So's my mother. She went after her prey, my father, like a falcon, and she caught him. Not that he resisted. He thinks he got the best of that deal. A beauty queen with smarts and a great life in Hong Kong where he gets to improve his Chinese every day. His Chinese is now better than my mother's. Anyway, she was my chaperone during my reign. Her plan is for me to marry well like she did. Well means smart and rich, of course. And to remain a virgin until my wedding night like she did. She made me practice looking down my nose at guys who would come on to me. She told me to act like I had an invisible shield around me. Like I'm too good for them. Honestly, it was like *The Princess Diaries*. My mom is a Chinese version of Julie Andrews. I told her I couldn't promise anything."

"How did she take it?"

"What can she do? She's a zillion miles away. She can't wait up for me, screen my dates if I had any, or do any matchmaking. Besides, she's the last person I'd ask for advice about anything sexual. Even kissing would be too dirty a topic for her."

"Really? Even just how to kiss? The whole 'close eyes, open lips, tilt head, run tongue over lips, kiss cheeks, trail your lips to his lips, open mouth but no tongue at first, make sure arms around partner' thing?"

"Oh, no, I mean well, yes, that kind of thing." Victoria felt silly sucking up the basics like a sponge, but how else was she going to learn? Anyway, this was Cindy. She wouldn't laugh at her for being hopelessly naïve.

"Well, my mom isn't here, so I can finally do what all the other girls are doing." As soon as she found out what that was. "She'll never know. She's got the family business to run while my dad writes up a new economic plan for Hong Kong. See what I've got to live up to?"

"You're lucky to have parents who care what you do. Irina,

my stepmom, cares that I'm around to be her slave, to help her run the spa, and that's about it."

"That sucks," Victoria said sympathetically.

"It's okay, I'm used to it," Cindy said brightly.

Victoria didn't know how Cindy coped with her nasty stepmother and those two vicious stepsisters who'd done their best to ruin Cindy's romance with Marco. She had guts, and so much determination to get what she wanted, Victoria was determined not to complain about her own situation ever again. At least not in front of Cindy.

She glanced out the floor-to-ceiling window to see that students were straggling in, sluggish after two weeks off. She searched the crowd for a tall blond boy but she didn't see him. Not the one she was looking for anyway.

She'd been counting the days until school started and it wasn't because she missed the academic challenge. Far from it. At least she'd see him last period in English. Unless he'd changed his schedule.

What would she say when she saw him? *How did you like the book? Did you have a good time skiing? Do you have a girlfriend I don't know about? It can't be that you're too busy or intimidated to ask me out, so what is it? Are you . . . just not that into me?*

She had to stop thinking about Steve so much. She not only needed lessons in kissing, she also needed basic flirting skills. How do you make it clear you're interested in someone without scaring them off? Was it true that when men want you, they'll find a way? How do you know if someone only likes you because you're rich and you were once a beauty queen? Fortunately here at Manderley almost everyone was rich and no one but Cindy knew she was Miss Junior Hong Kong. She turned back to her friend.

"So did you see Marco over the holidays?"

"He went back to Italy to have Christmas with his family, but he sent me this postcard." Cindy pulled out a hand-painted card with a photograph of houses spilling down the cliff toward the azure sea.

"Ohhh, is this where he lives?" Victoria turned the card over to see the message was in Italian. "What does he say?" she asked.

Cindy grinned. "Oh, just the usual. You know how Italians are."

"I don't think I do."

"They're very, uh, out there. I had to look up most of the words in my dictionary. I'm not sure whether my Italian is up to it."

"There's no question he's definitely into you," Victoria said. "If I met someone who looked like a Greek god and played soccer like a pro and wrote romantic postcards and who'd invited me to visit him in Italy next summer, I'd be willing to lose my virginity. I mean, what's it good for anyway?"

Victoria really wished someone would tell her. She was pretty sure she and Cindy were both still virgins. What were they waiting for? What would it take?

"Good question, Victoria."

That wasn't the answer Victoria was looking for. That wasn't an answer at all. She wanted to know if Cindy was having sex with Marco and should she, Victoria, offer herself to Steve. And if so, how?

Instead she rephrased the question. "What I want to know is do all American high school girls have sex? Does it matter who with? Or is it just important to do it by a certain age?"

"Yes, no, and yes," Cindy said.

"Well that's more than I learned at my last school. Of course it was an all-girls school so we were all in the dark."

"A girls school? I wouldn't like that," Cindy said.

"It's different. No one dresses up. We wore uniforms. No makeup. Why bother? For fun we'd get together on the weekends to have facials. Then I did everyone's hair for them. I'm pretty good at it actually." Victoria studied Cindy's deep red curly hair.

"Has anyone ever told you you have gorgeous hair?" Victoria asked.

"A few people," she said.

It was no surprise Cindy didn't realize how stunning her hair was or could be. Some days it looked like Cindy had barely combed it. If Victoria had hair that color she'd be wearing clothes in vivid colors. She'd wear her hair smooth and shiny, and that's not all she'd do.

"You could use a good shaping," Victoria said gently so as

not to hurt Cindy's feelings. "Why don't you let me cut it for you?"

Cindy self-consciously ran her hand through her hair. "Really? You wouldn't mind?"

"Are you kidding? I live for that kind of stuff—hair, clothes, jewelry, makeup."

"I don't wear makeup."

Victoria sighed. "I know, but you should. Just a touch. I can show you."

Then she leaned back in her chair. She was exhausted. She'd been up for hours. Now she had to go to math class when she'd much rather do a makeover for her friend. Her parents insisted she take advanced algebra even though she was terrible at math. Their path was for her to get an MBA at Harvard, then, after marrying some suitably ambitious man, come back to Hong Kong to participate in the family business. Victoria had other plans.